LOV

Dr. Gersper has ... spellbinding novel, based on the lives of his uncle and aunt, who, with luck and the help of others, overcame traumatic adversities and launched themselves along a path of happiness, success and eternal love.

The novel is both fascinating and exceptionally well-written. This is particularly amazing to me, not only because it is Dr. Gersper's first novel, but also because he recently celebrated his 80th birthday.

I'm certain that the story of the lives of Charlie and Molly will be an inspiration to anyone who reads it, because it shows that it's possible for two people to love each other, deeply and tenderly, for their entire lives. It also shows that personal redemption is possible; that personal responsibility is as important in our modern world as it was 100 years ago, and that it is important for everyone to live lightly on the land.

Love Letters from the Grave is a truly inspiring story, and I recommend it highly.

Dr. Frank Shankwitz
Creator and Co-Founder, Make-A-Wish Foundation
Honorary Doctor of Public Services

I got a chance to read Paul Gersper's first novel this weekend and I can't tell you how much I enjoyed it. On his first try as a novelist, Dr. Gersper has crafted a beautiful love story of two hopelessly romantic souls who find true love. I hope this inspires him to write many more.

Marshall Trimble
Official Arizona State Historian

LOVE LETTERS from THE GRAVE

A Novel

DR. PAUL GERSPER

Happy Living

Published in the United States by:
Happy Living Books Independent Publishers
www.happyliving.com/books

All of the characters and companies in this book are fictitious, and any resemblance to actual persons, living or dead, or companies is purely coincidental.

ISBN: 978-0-9972210-8-4

Copyright 2016 by Paul Logan Gersper

All rights reserved. Without limiting the rights under the copyright reserved above, no part of this publication may be reproduced, stored in, or introduced into a retrieval system, or transmitted in any form or by any means (electronic, mechanical, photocopying, recording, or otherwise) without prior written permission.

For permission requests, please contact:
matt@happyliving.com

Printed in the United States of America

Other books by Happy Living
_____

Turning Inspiration into Action (2016)
By Matt Gersper

The Belief Road Map (2016)
By Matt Gersper and Kaileen Elise Sues

Join our community to stay informed of upcoming books, promotions and updates from Happy Living! We are on a mission to improve the health and wellbeing of the world, one person at a time.

Our blog is filled with ideas for living with health, abundance, and compassion.

Go to www.happyliving.com to sign up for our free membership.

This book is dedicated to the love of my life, and my best friend, who for more than 60 years has kept me on an even keel, and has been an outstanding role model for our four children, ten grandchildren and four great-grandchildren. She is the nicest person I have ever known, and is the main reason our marriage has also been one made in heaven.

The book is also dedicated to my children Markham, Matthew, Linda, and Michael; all good citizens of the world; all successful in their own right, and all loved and admired by their parents.

Also to family veterans, including my father, Paul; my daughter, Linda; my son-in-law, Gary; and to those still serving, including my son, Michael, and grandsons, Markham and Jeffrey, who have done or are still doing their part to keep our country free.

Finally, it is dedicated to three of the finest teachers there ever were: my high school teacher, Irvin Rickly, who taught me the importance of thinking before speaking; my college major professor, mentor and friend, Nicholas Holowaychuk, who taught me how to think effectively and how to fearlessly and confidently tackle the most difficult of problems; and my university mentor, colleague and friend, Hans Jenny, who taught me how to think holistically, and to always conduct my research and teaching selflessly and within the context of improving the human condition as well as the condition of the earth and all its inhabitants.

*'I come to the garden alone, while the dew is still on the roses,
And the voice I hear, falling on my ear, the Son of God discloses.
And he walks with me, and he talks with me, and he tells me I am his own,
And the joy we share as we tarry there, none other has ever known ...'*

In the Garden, Molly's song for Charlie

You looked very beautiful tonight standing by the store room door. After you left, Danny asked me who the pretty girl was. I told him just a friend. I'd like to tell them all that you are my one and only."

Charlie's first love letter

Prologue

Meeting Luther, 1989

*Listen to me, mister. You're going to get back on that horse
and I'm going to be right behind you, holding on tight
and away we're going to go, go, go!*

Ethel, On Golden Pond

I didn't mean to follow him. It was just coincidence that led us to the same spot, on the same day, in the same unusual circumstances.

He was leaning on the fence, young and out of place, looking as if he'd rather be swimming across the lake, or - better yet - racing across it on water skis behind a motorboat. Anywhere, perhaps, than beside a field in a light drizzle.

Couldn't say I blamed him. I felt pretty much the same myself.

'Get a story,' my editor had told me. 'I want you to write about how the Amish are embracing the future.'

'Seriously?' It was hardly my usual fare, even for a local newspaper. 'What about the trail of violent robberies in the east of the county?'

Garner had sighed, sliding his glasses down his nose to peer at me. 'Brendon, you were nearly shot last time you insisted on investigating violent robberies. I don't need you off sick for four weeks with a hole in your leg. Or longer, with a hole in another part of you. Take the job, and relax.'

It was an order, and I knew it.

So I'd done what he said. I'd rented a car, got myself a cabin by the lake for a week, deep in Amish country, and packed a fishing rod. I might as well do something I enjoyed while I was stuck here, trying to interview a bunch of people who had no interest in being interviewed.

Like the guy at the fence.

I'd seen him over at the lake the previous evening, heaving boxes out of a neat blue coupe and depositing them in one of the nearby houses, chatting amiably with the elderly couple who seemed to own it. It looked like a scene from On Golden Pond. My own cabin, three buildings away, was very much more functional, but it would do for a few days. Its lack of inspiration matched my own.

I pulled up some distance from the young man, taking care not to scare the horse attached to the traditional vehicle behind him before I ambled over to join him.

'Car break down?' I jerked my head at the Amish buggy; it creaked gently as the glossy black mare between its prongs reached out for juicier grass by the fence post.

The man smiled. 'I'm just minding the buggy for my family while the barn-raising goes on. I said I'd wait to see if they need any spare hands.'

'They seem to be doing pretty well,' I said, leaning on the fence beside him and following his gaze. 'I'm Brendon, by the way.'

'Luther,' he replied, and shook my offered hand.

We both resumed our staring, watching the flurries of activity across the field as the Amish community set about adding a new building to their small township. My own forebears had built their house this way, centuries ago, so it should have interested me more, but it was the young man beside me, staring so intently at the smattering of wooden buildings, that had grabbed my attention. Despite the peaceful and relatively dull surroundings, interrupted only by occasional laughter or a shout of 'Hold it upright, Jacob!', my journalistic instincts were beginning to twitch.

There was a story here, for sure.

Why else would a young black man be minding an Amish buggy for his folks, who were nowhere to be seen in the bustling legions of cooks and builders ahead of us?

'So …' I said casually, pulling out my notebook. 'I'm a reporter with the joyful task of working out how the Amish are embracing the future. Do you have any suggestions as to where I should start? Maybe updating the transport.'

I nodded again to the buggy behind him.

For a moment, Luther took his eyes off the distant figure he was watching – a tall woman piling dishes onto one of the tables - and looked directly at me.

Then he laughed. 'I think the transport is completely appropriate,' he said evenly, with the considered speech of someone well accustomed to debating. 'Quiet, practical, and doesn't eat into our fossil fuel reserves. In fact,' he added, nodding to the little heap of manure behind the buggy, 'Black Beauty even makes her own fuel.'

'True.'

Interesting. Silently, I congratulated myself on my story-sniffing abilities. Not many guys his age could have spoken so confidently like that, or even thought like that. This young man was definitely worth talking to – might even save me a heap of investigation.

I'd be back at the cabin with a beer and a fishing rod in no time.

Luther confirmed this by continuing his little "save the world" lecture. 'Actually, they're embracing the future right now, by building a new home for their newlyweds. That's forward-looking, right?'

Now it was my turn to laugh. 'You've got me there. I can't see my son owning his own home for many decades. If he ever graduates from college, he'll be sleeping over the garage forever. So ... well, can you tell me what's going on here?'

'Sure. Sarah, who's nearly twenty,' he said, pointing out a smiling, blonde-haired young woman, 'is marrying Jacob.'

Ah. Jacob. The guy who was helping to straighten out the uprights.

'She and her husband are being feted with a two-day barn-raising celebration. When a couple marries, it's the obligation of the parents to set them up in the business of farming, providing them with a sizable piece of land and all the relevant building materials, animals, farming equipment, and furnishings. And then it's the obligation of the community to build the house, the barn, and the other out-buildings.'

'Over a weekend?'

It sounded impossible.

'Over a weekend,' said Luther. 'Three days at the most. Impressive, huh?'

I nodded, watching the barn-raising unfold with more intrigue, now that Luther could bring it to life for me.

'My family and I started with a hearty breakfast of ham, eggs, potatoes and biscuits at six am, then they boarded the buggy for the 8-mile drive while I drove behind. Molly had never before ridden in a horse drawn buggy, but Charlie said it brought back memories of his youth, living on his parent's farm.' Once again, Luther waved a hand at the distant crowds, but I still couldn't spot this Molly and Charlie he was referring to. 'Molly sat in the rear seat with Mary, Sarah's mother, while Charlie sat up front with Aaron, Sarah's father. He drove the horse at a pretty vigorous trot so they didn't take long to get here. And when we did – wow. We were absolutely amazed at the huge crowd of people milling about.'

I followed his gaze and did a few quick calculations. 'That's got to be two hundred men, women and children.'

'All sorted into groups for specific tasks and chores.' Luther grinned. 'I've only ever seen that level of organization on my family's mini-farm.'

It was like a military campaign, though admittedly the most peaceful one I'd ever seen. The men, all bearded, and dressed in black trousers, white shirts and black hats, were organized into skilled construction teams, each headed by an experienced elder. They laid the foundations, constructed the buildings, and did all the painting, both the exteriors and interiors of the buildings. The teenaged boys, without beards but dressed the same as the men, worked directly with these teams, providing labor while learning vital building skills. Even the youngest boys of four and five years old were assigned to the different teams, fetching tools, building materials and supplies as demanded by the various crews.

The women, meanwhile, all dressed in bonnets, dresses and aprons in combinations of blues and white, managed the catering. While the teenagers did the table settings and ran refreshments to the working men, the younger girls provided assistance to the older women and teenagers, and took care of the infants.

The oldest women stirred the vast pots and ran from their houses with hot bread in their aprons, including the tall, strawberry-haired lady whom Luther appeared to be watching most closely.

Even at this distance I could see that she was serenely beautiful, as upright as one of those timbers in spite of her advancing years. I recognised her as the woman from the lake house, the one with whom Luther had been chatting as he trailed his boxes into the house. Now she stretched for a moment, her hands in the small of her back as she glanced across the field toward the carpenters.

Then I saw him. The elderly gentleman from the lake house turned his head, his Amish clothing not able to disguise the solidity of his form, or his blunt, handsome features. It was as if he'd felt her watching; instantly he turned and raised a hand, giving her a rueful grin which she quickly returned. They were so much a part of the whole, but somehow they seemed to stand out amongst the other women in blue dresses and men garbed in black.

I tore my eyes back to Luther as he described what was happening.

'I joined them during the dinner break which was done in shifts,' he said. 'It was delicious - tender ham, and biscuits slathered with butter. Sarah came over and introduced us to Jacob, and Charlie wished them a marriage as happy, fruitful and successful as his and Molly's. I have to tell you, any couple would be lucky to have that. They sure are a pair.'

'But embracing the future,' I reminded him, thinking of Jacob and Sarah. 'Aren't the Amish all ... related? Surely that causes issues.'

Luther raised an eyebrow. 'I wondered about that too. But they've got that covered, apparently. This particular farming community stretches over a radius, from the town, of around twenty-five miles, and a large number of the people *are* related. However, to avoid birth defects in their babies they have a managed, proactive system of mutual immigration between Amish Communities throughout North America. Jacob's family immigrated here from an unrelated Amish Community in northern Mexico when Jacob was only ten.'

'So Jacob and Sarah aren't even distant cousins. Ingenious.'

'It really is,' agreed Luther. 'Planning well into the future.'

The evidence of all this ingenuity and sheer ... community ... was clear to see, and for a moment, I envied the simple productivity of it all, of how my own ancestors would have created our home. By evening, all the buildings would be erected, with only a bit of roofing remaining to be done. This, along with finishing the building interiors, doing the outside and inside painting, and completing some finishing touches, would be done on the second day, before turning the farmstead over to Jacob and Sarah. On the following day, as the final touches were being applied to the building, other Amish men and boys would fill the barn with hay, animal feed, animals and equipment, the house with furniture, curtains, drapery, linens, dinnerware, and utensils, and the outbuildings with tools and supplies.

'By the time everyone leaves tomorrow, Jacob and Sarah will have a home ready for occupancy and a farmstead ready for farming. Can you imagine?'

Luther shook his head, hardly able to take it in himself even though it was all transpiring before his eyes.

But surely he *should* be able to imagine that. 'Well, won't you get that, too, if your family is Amish?'

The young man turned to me with a frown. 'My family isn't Amish,' he said. 'They're African-Americans from North Carolina.'

'But you said—'

Suddenly his head jerked upwards. 'Oh, my aunt and uncle are coming.'

It was the Golden Pond couple, striding across the field toward us as quickly as the woman's long dress would allow.

'So who are they?' I asked, thoroughly confused by now.

'Those are my great-aunt and uncle, Molly and Charlie,' he said with a little twitch of his mouth.

He was enjoying this now, keeping me on the ropes.

I looked at them again, holding hands and laughing as Molly trod on the trailing hem of her skirt.

'Wait. That old Amish couple, who think a horse-drawn buggy is a Ferrari and have obviously been married forever, are your great-somethings?'

Luther shrugged. 'It's complicated,' he said with a mighty twinkle in his eye.

He knew exactly what he was doing. "It's complicated" was music to a journalist's ears. "It's complicated" meant there was a story here. A big, complex, interlaced story that was just the kind of fish I wanted to land.

'And they haven't been married forever,' added Luther mischievously. 'They only met when they were nearly forty years old, and both in happy marriages.'

Pulling the face of youth which suggested that forty was ancient, Luther clambered up into the buggy and reached for the reins. 'You're even wrong about the buggy,' he said in an infuriating drawl, like a child harboring an outrageous secret. 'They know all about fast vehicles. All about them. Do you like to drive fast, Brendon? I sure did.'

He was reeling me in, landing me right at his feet on the floor of an Amish buggy.

'You'd better tell me this story,' I told him. 'Otherwise my boss won't need to worry about me getting shot, because I'm going to die of plain old curiosity.'

At least he had the humility to laugh at my perplexed expression. I sighed, and handed him my card.

'Start talking,' I told him. 'And soon.'

'I've got all weekend,' he said, nodding across to the barn-raising, 'if you have the time to spare.'

And suddenly the blank wooden walls of my lake-side cabin seemed a whole lot more interesting.

Chapter 1

Charlie Boy

They used to tell me I was building a dream,
And so I followed the mob.
When there was earth to plow or guns to bear
I was always there, right on the job.

Brother, Can You Spare a Dime, Al Jolson

The Great Depression, they were calling it. What was so great about it, Charlie had no idea.

But then, he knew they weren't suffering so badly, out in the countryside with all the home-grown produce and stock they had to hand. In the city, he'd heard Mr Edmundson saying in church the previous week, there was all sorts of lawlessness, what with people starving and all, unable to find work or even a crust to eat.

They had plenty of crusts here on the farm. Which was a very good job, because there were a lot of mouths to feed. And sometimes Charlie felt like it was his personal responsibility to feed every single one of them.

Like all the other farming folk in the area, children provided much of the labor required by their farming operation. At the age of three, Charlie had joined his three older brothers in routinely doing chores - helping his mother around the house and his father around the farm. By the time he was six, he had a four-year old sister who was given the responsibility of assisting their mother with chores inside the house, while he and his next oldest brother did most of their mother's outside chores - cutting and stacking firewood; managing the goat herd of twelve or so animals to keep the very large lawn "mowed" by rotating the stakes; milking the goats and the milk cows; feeding the chickens, ducks and rabbits, and watering the livestock.

No sooner had he mastered all that, than he'd reached the age and size that meant he was expected to take care of the farm's horses and mules. Along with learning to work the draft animals, he was also taught how to operate, maintain and use the farm's gasoline-engine-powered machinery and vehicles. He turned over his previous chores of maintaining the goat herd and cows to his next youngest brother. By this time his parents had nine children - seven boys and two girls.

And then they moved another family in.

Walter and Jewel and their four children took up residence in an old house on the farm, Walter working hard to keep the farm's buildings in good repair and Jewel pitching in with the house-keeping. They were good friends from the church, and mostly good to have around.

The not-so-good part was Walter and Jewel's son, Wendell. There weren't many who believed that Wendell was good to have around.

Charlie could see Wendell now, carrying out his favorite past-time of doing nothing-in-particular-apart-from-no-good. Right at that moment, as Charlie raced between his chores around the farm and school, where he was excelling right now, and the church which had been a haven for his whole life, it irked him just a tiny bit to see that Wendell was back, stretched out on the veranda of his parents' house as if he owned it.

'Home from your travels, Wendell?' he called, panting only a little as he ran toward the bigger house in the corner of the farm, by the county road.

Wendell didn't comment. He never did comment when anyone asked where he'd been on his little trips away. He ran off, upset his parents, came back, upset his parents. The pattern was always the same, until the day they'd told him to leave for good until he could sort himself out. Presumably, he'd done some sorting.

Wendell simply stared at him with narrowed eyes, then nodded. 'Hey, Charlie,' he called after a moment. 'What are you running for?'

'I've got news!'

Charlie held up his school books in explanation, even though that wouldn't mean much to the older boy. School and Wendell hadn't really agreed with each other, once he'd got in with the wrong crowd and stopped being the model student he used to be.

'We should go for a drive later. Celebrate your good news,' shouted Wendell.

Charlie grinned as he skidded toward the back door. That might even be fun. Heck, any kind of driving was fun, and the faster the better, though his recent racing attempts had brought attention from law-enforcement officers and, even worse, from their neighbors, who began to lodge complaints to his parents that he was endangering children and livestock with his fast driving. Charlie knew they were right, and vowed that he would be extra careful to slow down to a safe speed when he spotted youngsters or animals, or passed through areas where they would most likely to be on the road.

But a quiet lane, a backroad, with Wendell urging him on – well, that could be arranged.

The screen door banged behind him as he ran into the house. 'Mom, Dad! Are you here? I've got something to tell you!'

His mother appeared from the kitchen, wiping her hands on her apron. 'Goodness, that sounds exciting. Your father is fixing the tractor. Why don't you go and help him?'

'Well, I am better with machinery than he is,' said Charlie with a cheeky grin.

'I meant so that you could tell him your news first.' As hard as his mother tried to sound affronted, she couldn't hide her smile. 'Go on, off with you.'

'Don't you want to know what it is?'

'I'll hear it later.'

Grabbing an apple in the orchard, Charlie set off at a trot again, wending his way across the farm to the tractor shed from where the sounds of clanging metal and muffled curses were emanating.

'Dad, I have something to tell you,' he cried triumphantly.

'You crashed into something?' Wielding a large wrench, Charlie's father was striking half-heartedly at a bent fender in an attempt to stop it slicing through the tire.

Charlie took the wrench off him. 'No; no crashing involved,' he said, levering the fender toward him rather than driving it further toward the rubber tire as his father had been doing. 'Mr Carter, the farm advisor, has recommended to the school that I take the 4-H program. It'll help me with my university application so I can go ahead and get my science degree.'

'And what are you going to do with that?'

'I'll be a new kind of farmer, working with the university agricultural experiment station, and …' He thwacked the very end of the fender with the wrench, and it curled obediently into place. '… I'll be able to do research and development right here on the farm.'

His father watched him carefully as Charlie tweaked the plugs and then turned the ignition on. The tractor burst into life and moved forward easily, now that its tire was free from impending death.

'I don't know, Charlie boy,' he said eventually. 'What happened to being a priest?'

That had been Charlie's calling for the previous few years.

'I can still love the Lord and work His land,' said Charlie. 'I know I've spent all these years studying with Father Patton at the church and doing extra lessons with the nuns at school, and I won't stop doing that. But this way I can be home, and help out with the farm, and even grow it toward greater things.'

'That's a lot of responsibility for a fifteen-year old, son,' said his father solemnly. 'You do so much around the farm and the church already, taking care of the family and all as well as your school work. Are you sure you can fit anything else in?'

Charlie held the wrench out beseechingly, like some kind of communion offering. 'I'm sure I can. I mean, Mr Carter wouldn't have recommended me for the program if he didn't think I could do it.'

His father drew in an enormous breath, as if pondering the puzzles of the universe. Then he winked.

'Well, I guess I wouldn't have recommended the 4-H to Mr Carter in the first place if I didn't think you could manage,' he said. 'We're very proud of you, Charlie boy, and I think it's an opportunity you can't miss.'

Charlie laughed, pumping his father's outstretched hand. 'Thank you!'

'I don't want you to burn yourself out, though, especially while school is in session. You'll need transport to get to and from home, school and church as fast as possible.'

'I have Betsy.'

For nearly a year, Charlie had been using the old saddle horse to get around, but this had the drawback of needing to have a place to keep the horse, as comfortably as possible, while at the school and church, and it also took time to unsaddle and saddle the horse at the terminus. He wasn't about to complain to his parents, however. Whatever it took to keep his folks lined up with the notion of additional studies, he would suffer it.

'Oh! Well, if Betsy's working out okay, I'll send the car back,' said his father casually, taking the wrench from Charlie and turning his back to put it into the toolbox.

Charlie's heart quickened. 'Car? What car?'

Charles Senior allowed himself a small smile that Charlie couldn't miss, before pointing out through the double doors. 'That Essex roadster out there.'

Charlie raced outside. The sleek, cream-colored car was parked outside, engine idling. It was a wonder he hadn't heard it. The Essex was very similar to the one which his oldest brother, William, had purchased a few months earlier. Charlie could hardly believe he was being given something that his own much-revered big brother had had to buy for himself.

'My own car?' he whispered.

'Unless you don't want it,' replied his father.

He needed no further encouragement. With a whoop of joy, Charlie dived behind the wheel and roared along the farm tracks, taking very great care not to run over so much as a bug as he opened the engine and headed for the open road. Life just got sweeter with every mile, and Charlie could almost feel the future unfolding before him like the tracks beneath the roadster's wheels – effortless, top-speed, free as a bird that had just unfurled its wings. The world was his oyster. No, the *pearl* in the oyster. And Charlie was ready to find that treasure. His fortune. His life.

Later that week as he was leaving the schoolhouse, Charlie found Wendell standing at the foot of the steps waiting for him. He hadn't spoken to Wendell at any length for quite some time; in fact, he had barely talked to him at all since his parents kicked him out of their home.

At closer quarters, Charlie could see that there was something different about Wendell – a kind of confidence that he hadn't had before. Perhaps it was a result of being older. Wendell was eighteen already, a young man rather than a boy reaching for adulthood. Furthermore, Wendell was very well-dressed, and appeared to be successful in whatever he was doing to earn a living.

'Charlie boy!' he called in an unusually enthusiastic manner.

Yep, definitely different.

'You didn't come around for a drive the other night.'

'Oh, sorry, Wendell. I forgot. Went clean out of my head when I got my new car.'

Wendell nodded knowingly. 'You got that cream-colored Essex roadster, right?'

Without waiting for Charlie to reply, the older lad seized Charlie by the shoulders and spun him around. 'Nice little ride, the Essex. But I've got me a real car.'

It was parked across the street: a huge, brand new, shiny black Packard. It truly was an impressive vehicle, and made Charlie a little weak at the knees in a way that not even his own roadster had accomplished.

'Want to take a ride with me?'

'Are you kidding? Yes!'

Charlie could barely keep still in the passenger seat, so enraptured was he with the power and beauty of the Packard. They thrummed their way through the streets, turning heads as they went, until they hit the quieter roads that reached their pale fingers out into the lush, green countryside.

A little way out of town, Wendell cruised to a halt.

'Would you like to drive?'

Charlie, who'd already had the experience of driving his father's large, late model, four-door Ford Sedan a few times, agreed in moments, scrambling across to the driver's seat and expertly adjusting it to give himself the best driving position. After a few minutes of driving, Wendell suggested that they take a road which was seldom travelled, and open her up. Charlie was amazed and thrilled with the power, speed and handling of the car. He had never driven so fast!

It was over too soon, but before it became too dark for Charlie to do his chores he had to drive back to the drug store. He and Wendell chatted briefly over a chocolate malt, before agreeing to meet again at the same place the following Sunday. As Charlie drove his beloved Essex roadster home, he couldn't help feeling disloyal, as if he'd cheated on her with a fancier model.

The week passed unremarkably and incredibly slowly, with the prospect of driving the Packard again dangling temptingly before Charlie. He arrived at the drugstore as soon as he could after church and supper, only to find that Wendell was already there. He had with him an older man, who appeared to be in his mid-thirties. They were standing on the sidewalk in front of the drugstore next to not one, but two identical Black Packards which were parked along the curb.

Charlie forced himself not to stare at the cars, but to concentrate instead on greeting the older man.

'This is my boss, Mr Hepworth,' said Wendell. Hepworth took Charlie's hand and nodded curtly. 'Mr Hepworth has a job that you might be interested in doing.'

Over malts in the drug store, Charlie explained that he was too busy to take on another job, trying not to notice that Mr Hepworth was staring at him the whole time. 'I have chores all around the farm, and scriptures with Father Patton, and that's besides the extra studies I've just taken on.'

Hepworth spoke for the first time, his speech as pinched as his sallow face. 'I'm only interested in hiring you for a few hours on a week-day morning to drive the second Packard.'

'Oh. Well, that might be okay, I guess.'

'I will pay you $100 for those few short hours. The date is Friday next.' Hepworth shrugged, as if it didn't matter either way to him. He obviously had other people lined up for the job. 'You'll have to decide quickly.'

With that, he drained his malt and left the drugstore, before Charlie could even tell him that he'd consider it carefully.

'He's very … um …' Charlie couldn't think how to describe the man to Wendell – certainly not without offending him.

'Clever,' finished Wendell. 'He's brilliant. That's why he's planning the job.'

His eyes narrowed as he spoke, as if he, too, were weighing Charlie up.

'So … what is the job?'

Wendell glanced around before leaning in close to Charlie. 'It's a bank robbery.'

'What?'

'The boss and the gang are planning a robbery in the city, and he wants the two of us – you and me, Charlie boy – to drive the two Packards as get-away cars.'

'I … I don't want to be part of a bank robbery.'

'You won't!' said Wendell smoothly. 'Nobody's going to get hurt, and nobody will get caught, and anyway, the drivers aren't part of the actual robbery. You won't be exposed to any danger, or any criminal liability. It's just a drive, Charlie. A super-fast, super-exciting car ride.'

'I don't …' He couldn't think straight. 'I can't …'

'Hey, Charlie.' Wendell moved in even closer so that Charlie was staring into his dilated pupils. 'I recommended you to the boss. I told him what an excellent driver you are. You're not going to let me down and make me look stupid, are you?'

Charlie shook his head, trying to get his thoughts straight. A hundred bucks for some exciting driving was quite an offer. Hard to ignore. But a bank robbery …

'Don't worry about it, Charlie,' whispered Wendell. 'These robberies are a dime a dollar since the Depression started. It's true. Hell, bank-robbing gangs are being celebrated as folk heroes by huge swathes of the American people. Think of it this way: it's just the poor folk taking back what the stockbrokers stole from us.'

'So … so it's almost like helping the people who've suffered,' said Charlie uncertainly.

'Exactly.' Wendell counted out a couple of dollars to pay for the malts, as if to show Charlie just what the poor could achieve when they put their minds to it. 'And there's no danger, remember? You just think about it, while we take the Packard for a spin.'

Charlie agonized over the offer as he nosed the car out through town. His first inclination was to turn it down, for rational and obvious reasons. However, he could use the $100. That would help out around the farm so much. He could try some of the new innovations that the County Farm Advisor was suggesting. It was easy money, and it could do some good in any number of ways.

And he very much wanted to experience the thrill of driving that fast, powerful Packard at full throttle. For two hours, Charlie drove Wendell around the countryside in the big car, taking every opportunity to accelerate, speed, and maneuver it around all manner of obstacles. Once again, he was amazed - elated, even - with how well the car performed.

'Okay,' he said, as they pulled up near the Essex so he could drive himself home. 'I'll do it.'

Wendell smiled, staring out through the windshield at the road ahead of them.

'See?' he said softly. 'I knew you were a smart boy. That's why I recommended you for the job. I knew you wouldn't let me down.'

'I wouldn't,' Charlie assured him. 'I mean, I won't. I've given you my word, and you can rely on me, Wendell.'

Even at fifteen years old, Charlie knew that to be true. Charlie was an achiever. He got things done.

And he'd never let anyone down in his life.

Chapter 2

The Folk Hero

"After two years I remember the rest of that day, and that night and the next day, only as an endless drill of police and photographers and newspaper men ... Most of the reports were a nightmare – grotesque, circumstantial, eager, and untrue."

The Great Gatsby, F Scott Fitzgerald

The 4-H agricultural program had come in handy already, just a few short weeks into his studies. Charlie had arranged with his teachers and his parents to miss school on the Friday of the planned robbery, telling them he needed the time to do field work on his 4-H project.

'What about your chores, son?' asked his father. 'I know your program's important, but the farm has to come first.'

Charlie smiled, hoping he looked more calm than he felt. 'I've done some of them early. As for the rest ... well, I'll be home in plenty of time.'

And now he had time to kill. Maybe a minute - or more? It was impossible to tell.

He'd been both nervous and excited when he left home early on the Friday morning of the caper, driving away into the unknown. As arranged, he'd met Wendell early and driven to a planned location at the edge of the city to pick up the six gang members. They'd then driven, four to a Packard, to the targeted bank.

'Stay in the car,' snapped Hepworth to Charlie as he nodded to the three men in the back of the car. 'Don't move for anything or anyone until we're back. Understand?'

'Yes, sir,' said Charlie, his legs turning to liquid so fast that he doubted he could move anyway, even if he wanted to.

He'd heard about bank robberies, of course – it was impossible not to. As Wendell had said, they were becoming almost commonplace since the Wall Street Crash. But in Chicago. Not here. Somehow he'd never imagined he might be involved in one.

It had suddenly become very real when he saw the gun protruding from the pocket of one of the men in the back seat, and had watched Hepworth slip back the safety catch on a pistol as he climbed out of the car.

He wished he could talk to Wendell. He could ask if Wendell was armed, what they should do if anything went wrong. Charlie wasn't armed himself, and never would have been. He would have refused to even be a driver if he'd had even an inkling of what was to come. Wouldn't he? It was hard to think straight as adrenaline surged around his body.

Sitting at the wheel of the shiny black, late model, souped-up Packard, he tingled with a strange mix of excitement and anticipation that was tinged with a growing sense of dread. He assumed that Wendell, in an identical car parked in front of him, was feeling the same way. To settle his nerves, Charlie focussed on using his driving skills and love for speed to make a quick and successful get-away from the bank, picturing the gear changes, the stabs of his feet on the accelerator, the brakes, the twists and turns that he'd practiced with Wendell.

It was now several seconds – only seconds? – since they had pulled up to the curb at the side of the bank, watching as the six other members of their group marched briskly around the corner to enter the front door of the bank. Any moment now they would emerge from around the corner, hopefully carrying bags of money.

'Any moment now,' whispered Charlie. 'Any moment. They'll come out, with the money. The poor folks' money. Any second, Charlie.'

He'd convinced himself so much of this that he was just about to turn over the ignition, when a terrible sound emerged from the bank – a scream, followed by one, two, three gunshots, rapidly fired. Through the partially-opened windows Charlie could hear a woman sobbing, wailing to be spared, to be saved for her children's sake, and just as he was taking in what she was saying an explosion rang out, assaulting his ears. More sounds: an iron gate clanging shut – or open, it was impossible to tell; screaming, crying, a terrible howling like a keening stag, wounded but not killed, and then another gunshot. The keening stopped abruptly.

Charlie clutched his head between his hands, half as an attempt to cut out the horrible noises, half in horror and shock at where he'd found himself. What should he do? He was under the strictest orders not to get out for anyone, but he wanted to stop it, wanted to help the screaming woman, wanted to cry out to Wendell, to Hepworth, to anyone …

But his instructions had been very, very explicit. 'Do not move, not for anything or anyone. Wait until we come out.'

And as long as he sat there, unarmed, just driving a car, only driving a car, he wasn't part of this, was he? He was separate from it. Just a chauffeur. Just a fifteen-year old boy, thrilled at the chance to drive a flash car at top speed. Wasn't he? Charlie's breath caught in his throat. It was hard to inhale. Hard to think.

Suddenly, a vast number of police and unmarked cars raced in, seemingly from every direction, sliding to a screeching stop in a tight angle along the front and side of the bank. Armed men poured from the cars, some in police uniforms and some in civilian clothes, dropping instantly into defensive positions around the bank. A plain-clothed man behind a Ford Model A (and how could he take the time to know it was a Ford Model A? Charlie felt as though his brain was operating outside of his body) lined up his sights on the bank door and then gave a tiny but firm nod.

Almost immediately a cacophony of gunfire, shouting and screaming erupted, with men running heedlessly in all directions and horrific sounds of all kinds bouncing off the walls, the cars, the windows of the bank.

Bullets hit the car, tearing into the metal and glass and ricocheting off the Packard in front. Charlie dived onto the floorboard, covering his ears, cowering beneath the dash as the shouting, screaming and gunfire seemed to go on forever. Bullets sliced through the bodywork into the car, ripping through the padded ceiling and collecting in the driver's seat where, only moments ago, he'd been sitting, rigid with fear and indecision.

He lay shaking, coiled like a wolf pup. Suddenly both front doors were flung open, several pairs of hands reached in and Charlie was yanked violently out of the car. He turned to cry out to Wendell, to warn him that he should move, but through the linked arms of the two policemen who were hauling him toward their vehicle, still dodging bullets as whoever remained of the bank robbers fought back, Charlie saw something terrible – so terrible he knew it would remain with him for the rest of his life.

Wendell was exactly where he was meant to be: bolt upright in the driver's seat, waiting for Hepworth and the others to pile into the car. One side of his scalp was missing, and the whole of Wendell's face, still frozen into a shocked expression, was obscured by the curtain of blood that flooded over his features.

'Wendell,' whispered Charlie, hardly knowing the man, really, yet hardly able to take in, now, that he was dead, that Charlie would also be dead if he hadn't ducked below the dash, and that the whole robbery had gone very, very wrong indeed. 'You should have—'

'Shut your mouth, boy, or I'll shoot you myself,' hissed a voice in his ear.

A fist pounded against his temple. Charlie reeled, helpless. In a daze, he was flung up against the wall of the bank, frisked, and dragged to a paddy wagon.

He was only vaguely aware of his body being battered, bruised and lacerated by the cold, hard surfaces of the police vehicle as he was man-handled into its yawning darkness. He was stunned - rendered almost insensible by the ferocity of the attack on him and the other members of the gang. His head was spinning, his world violently turned upside down.

As the paddy wagon screamed toward the police station, he tried to figure out what had gone wrong. Where were the other members of the gang? His mind raced a mile-a-minute as he sped toward the unknown, alone in the paddy wagon apart from the law-enforcement officer, who wiped blood from his face with the back of his hand, glaring, and held the butt of his gun a few inches from Charlie's head throughout the journey.

Charlie shook his head, trying not to cry. He was supposed to be intelligent. He was an honors student, a 4-H participator. And yet he had given no thought to any of the consequences which might be associated with robbing banks. He had not even thought of himself as a member of the gang, simply a skilled driver and lover of speed. A hired hand. Although he was only 15-years-old, he was big for his age and much more mature than other boys of his age. He might look as old as Wendell, but the truth was, he was just a kid. And now he was headed to who knew where?

He was headed to jail. Thrown into a holding cell with two drunken vagrants who'd been caught in a brawl, scrapping over the ownership of a coat they'd found hanging on a fence, Charlie curled himself into a corner and tried to quell the uncontrollable shaking in his limbs. Shock was causing his system to shut down: shock at what had gone on, shock and outrage at himself that he hadn't thought this through properly. He ducked the flailing arms of his cellmates, who were still battling out the fate of a coat that was long gone, gulping back sobs.

Through the fog that had engulfed his mind, Charlie heard his name being called. He looked up, expecting to see the sheriff who had manhandled him so roughly into the jail before disappearing to have his wounds attended to. The sheriff was certainly standing beside the metal gate, but it was the man beside him who was calling out Charlie's name.

'You don't look like a bank robber,' he said now, loosening his tie and wafting his hat in front of his face. The air was pretty stagnant in the jail.

'I'm not a bank robber,' said Charlie, hardly able to push his words out. 'I'm a … just a driver. I was only driving. It wasn't meant …' He stopped short, afraid he wouldn't be able to hold back his tears if he continued, so determined was he to act like the man everyone had assumed he was. The man he was yet to be.

'We'll have to let the judge decide whether you're a bank robber or not, boy.' The man with the hat fanned himself again as he looked Charlie up and down. 'Either way, you're in a mighty pickle.' He sighed, then gestured to the sheriff to open up the door. 'My name is Adams. The court has assigned me as your public defender.'

'You're a … a lawyer?'

Adams nodded, his face somber, then led the way into a small, featureless office that was only marginally more cheerful than the jail cell.

'I was just driving,' said Charlie again, taking the seat that Adams pointed to. 'I didn't hurt anyone. Why do I need a lawyer?'

Placing his hat carefully on the table, Adams sighed deeply, then read aloud from a scribbled list that he'd extracted from his pocket.

'The attempted robbery turned out to be an incredible blood bath. The other ... driver ...' Adams paused to let the word sink in. 'He's dead. Five of the other members of the gang were killed at the site. The oldest member of the gang, the ringleader, Hepworth, was seriously wounded. He's being treated in the prison hospital. He'd better hope he dies there, because he's headed for the electric chair if he makes it out alive.'

Charlie stared at the table, his eyes burning with tears. Six members of the gang, dead. Wendell killed. Hepworth dying or nearly dead. He was the only one to make it out unharmed. How could this all have happened?

'The ... the woman,' he whispered. 'I could hear a lady screaming. What ... what happened?'

'Mrs Olsen.' Adams was once again reading from his list with a calmness that wasn't reflected in his sad, wary eyes. 'A customer. An innocent bystander. Yes, she was killed at the bank, along with ...' He totted up the names on his list with agonizing slowness. '... four police officers, two detectives and two of the bank's employees. Moreover, in addition to your gang's leader, three police officers, three detectives, two customers, the bank guard and the bank manager were wounded. So that's ... what, fifteen people killed and eleven people wounded. That makes it one of the bloodiest crime events in the entire country since the Crash. I hope you're proud of yourself, boy.'

Charlie shook his head, tears spilling down his cheek, numbed and confused by the carnage wrought during the attempted bank robbery. It was surreal - like a bad dream. It was almost impossible to believe that it had happened and that he was a part of it. He had not even thought of himself as a member of a "gang." And he certainly had not given a single thought to what consequences might result from robbing the bank. After all, he and Wendell were simply drivers of the get-away cars, and, unlike the other six members of the gang, were not even armed.

'I was just the driver,' he repeated. 'I only wanted to drive the Packard.'

Adams watched him sadly. 'How old are you, Charlie?'

'Fifteen, sir.'

'Fifteen.' The man swallowed hard. 'Well, you may be young but you will be tried as an adult. There is no question of you not being convicted for your part in this horrific crime, even if you were only the driver, in your view. Moreover—' Adams swallowed again, clearly finding this harder than his demeanor suggested. 'Moreover, you will almost assuredly be given the death sentence. There is absolutely no point in hoping for a different result. That gang of yours caused the deaths of six law-enforcement officers and three innocent bystanders. You cannot hope to avoid being executed in the electric chair, sometime before the end of the year.'

Charlie slumped into his chair. It was a living nightmare, and then when it ended he would go to Hell, where he belonged.

'But I didn't do anything,' he cried in anguish. 'I was just the driver. I didn't know those men; I didn't know what I was doing. It was just ... just for the car and a hundred bucks.'

Adams could barely meet his eye. 'You may believe that, Charlie,' he said eventually, 'and even I may believe that, but no judge or jury in the land is going to acquit you just because you didn't know what you were doing. You're going to the chair, son, and you'd better get used to the idea.'

Son. The word echoed around his brain. His father – Charles Senior. He'd know what to do. He'd believe his own son, the heir he trusted with running and expanding the farm.

'Can I speak to ... can't my father be brought here?'

Adams exchanged glances with the sheriff who was leaning in the doorway, then consulted his scrap of paper again. He directed his words to the table, unable to look at Charlie.

'Your father was brought here and told what you'd done. He was asked if he'd like to see you.' Adams chewed his lip. 'I'm afraid that he did not wish to see you. His exact words, I think, were that he has one son called William, who is working in the city, and five others back on the farm. He has no other son. No son called Charlie.'

'He ... he left?' He'd gone without speaking to Charlie. Without helping him. But surely he must know that Charlie would never do anything like this if he'd known what he was doing? Surely? 'Please! Get him to come back.'

Adams shook his head, that sad expression haunting his eyes again. 'He's disowned you, Charlie. I think you broke his heart. You're on your own now.'

The trial was over in three days. Charlie sat with his eyes downcast throughout, unable to work out how this nightmare had overtaken his life – was about to end his life. An empty chair stood to one side of him, as Hepworth was too injured to attend the trial. To his right sat Mr Adams, quiet and measured, carefully taking notes and gently propping Charlie up whenever the pain of hearing about the murders at the bank threatened to topple him.

The prosecuting attorney presented a short, concise, straight-forward case, in which he asked the jury to return a verdict of guilty and a recommendation of the death penalty for both the surviving bank robbers. Charlie shook his head silently. Just a driver. Not even a regular driver – just doing someone he barely knew a favor, for the excitement of driving a Packard.

Hepworth was quickly convicted and sentenced to die in the electric chair, with the sentence to be carried out immediately upon his release from the prison hospital.

Then it was Charlie's turn.

Adams tightened his tie and positioned himself solidly in the center of the court room.

'Members of the jury, I appeal to you for leniency in the case of my client. He has been painted as a member of this notorious gang, and yet here he is … just a boy. The day before the awful events at the bank, Charlie helped around the farm as he always did, doing many of his father's chores for him, as he has always done. He took care of his young siblings. He visited the church to talk with the priest and the nuns, who all adore and admire Charlie. Then he went to the high school where he is held up as an example to the other children, not of the things to avoid in this life, but of the way to be an exemplary student, on the way to university.'

A few members of the jury cast glances in Charlie's direction, but he stared down at his hands, unable to meet their eyes, hardly able to believe himself that what Mr Adams said was true. He chanced a glance behind him, and wished he hadn't. His mother sat five rows behind, held up by William, clutching a handkerchief to her tear-soaked cheeks. Of his father, there was no sign.

Adams had paused for his plea to sink in, but now he continued.

'This young man has no previous criminal record. In fact, he has no previous criminal connections whatsoever, apart from his unfortunate acquaintance with Wendell Harrison - which only came about because of the charity Charlie's family had extended to Harrison's folks, offering them a house on their farm. Charlie has only ever seen the best in people. The best of people. The best kind of people. He had no way to see through Harrison's manipulation of an innocent.'

Adams pointed at Charlie, and the jury's eyes followed his finger. 'He was recruited by the gang exclusively to be a get-away car driver. He was not armed. He did not participate in the robbery nor in the shoot-out. Did he know he was getting involved in a bank robbery? Yes, of course. He's a bright young man. But did he know what that meant, or what it could lead to? Not in any way whatsoever. That was so far from the life that Charlie had led up to that terrible day that he could not ever have foreseen what might happen. He should not die because of this, and you all know that. You have children of your own. You were young yourselves. You can see how this might have happened, even when Charlie wasn't able to see it for himself. If you truly care about justice, you will not give this boy the death sentence.'

Adams nodded firmly, first at the jury and then toward Charlie, and took his seat. When their arms touched, Charlie could feel the lawyer shaking.

'Thank you,' he whispered.

'Please don't thank me, Charlie,' replied the attorney under his breath as the jury were led from the room. 'I feel useless. You shouldn't be here at all. You shouldn't have been *there* at all. If I can save you from the chair, you can thank the good Lord for putting off the day of your meeting, and then spend every day of your life doing some good and showing your gratitude. But please, don't thank me.'

As it turned out, though, Charlie owed him a debt of gratitude which he could never forgot. Only minutes later, the jury returned, and Charlie stood to hear the death sentence.

The leader of the jury spoke directly to the judge. 'We return a verdict of guilty with extenuating circumstances, and recommend a sentence of life imprisonment instead of the death penalty.'

The gavel fell, and Charlie's fate was decided.

And so, a few days before his 16th birthday, Charlie left normal life far behind, and was faced instead with the traumatic uncertainty of spending the rest of his days in prison.

Chapter 3

A Popular Girl

They treated me like my poor heart was made of a rock or stone, Mama,
Made of a rock or stone.
Treated me like my poor heart was made of a rock or stone,
And that's no way for me to get along

That's No Way to Get Along, Robert Wilkins

Molly laughed as her nephew poked the cat with a branch. 'She'll only take that for so long, you know, Eddie,' she cried. 'Then you'll be sorry you provoked her.'

'What's prodoked?'

Eddie was toying idly with the stick, so she eased it gently out of his chubby hand.

'Teasing her. It's not right to tease people.'

'Or cats?'

Molly laughed again. 'Or cats.'

Their conversation drew Maureen out onto the porch. She leaned in the doorway, watching her younger sister guiding her son through some animal husbandry.

'You're a fine one to talk about teasing people, Molly,' she said with a smile, resting her hand on her growing belly.

Molly squinted up at her. 'I'm sure I don't know what you mean.' Her tone – and the way her freckled cheeks colored up pink - suggested that she knew exactly what her sister was implying.

'Hmm. Well, how many boys are you dating right now?'

'Just ... I don't know, four or five.' Molly shrugged. 'It's nothing serious – just ice cream parlors and county fairs.'

'There are a lot of county fairs around here. That's a lot of …'

'Ice cream,' interrupted Molly. 'That's all it is. Ice cream and a bit of fun.'

'What do Mom and Dad think of that?'

'They're fine. I'm not coming home with the local miscreants, you know.' Molly taunted her with an easy grin. 'These are nice boys, and they always approve. Get me home by ten pm and everything.'

Maureen's eyebrows knitted together. 'You've been graduated for a year and a half now. Isn't it about time you thought about settling down? I was married with a baby on the way at your age.'

'Yes, but you'd met Angus at my age. There's no Angus for me. Not here, anyways.'

'You'll find one,' said Maureen, herding Eddie out of the chicken pen. 'There's an Angus for you somewhere.'

'And until there is, I'll just keep dating and having fun.'

Molly waved them into the house, away from the flies and the squawk of the outraged chickens. Behind her sister's back, she blew out her cheeks. She was young still. There was no need to settle down. She liked walking out with her young men on a Sunday, being treated like a princess with no expectations other than a peck on the lips from any of them.

And anyway, where on earth would she find someone to settle down with?

She'd been born into a large family in a very small town, a town in which everyone not only knew each other, but also kept track of everyone else's business and activities. Molly's mother, Martha, and father, Jesse, had four sons as well as their daughters, and had lost another son to premature birth before Molly came along. The family also had a huge number of close relatives living all around: in their own town; in many nearby villages and communities, or on small farms across the area. Her father had always been employed in law-enforcement, first as a policeman in the largest town in the county, and then as deputy sheriff until finally he was elected as the County Sheriff. Her mother was a typical housewife, taking very good care of her husband, her six children, and the household. Her mother also served on the PTAs of her children's schools, and was very active in the social and political affairs of their community.

Sometimes it was hard to know where the family ended and the town began.

Right from elementary school, it had appeared that everyone was either a close or distant cousin. In junior high and high school, most of the students were in some way related to her. It made the prospect of dating seem fraught with danger. It seemed inevitable to Molly that she would one day become another cell in the organism of her family, merging with another part of the town so that it would then be her family too – just as Maureen had done. But she wasn't going to do it until she was sure she wasn't marrying anyone she was related to.

Somehow, this had made her a little irresistible to the boys at school. Maybe it was simply because she wasn't interested in settling down, while most of her female friends had set their hats at someone and their hearts on marriage at an early age. Either that, or it was her unexpected prowess with a baseball. Academically, Molly was an average student, but she was quite above average in extra-curricular activities. She never missed a ball game or any other school function, and from being drafted onto the boys' teams from the moment they'd seen her bat, she was very popular, even if she was a little shy. By graduation she had grown into a very attractive young woman - tall and slender, and with an easy, infectious smile.

She knew she was lucky, too. Although she graduated from high school during the depths of the Great Depression, she - along with her family, friends and nearly everyone else in the area - did not suffer like many other people around the country, particularly compared to those who lived in urban areas. While people who lived in urban areas suffered from very high unemployment rates, hunger, food shortages, and other deprivations, those in rural small town America did not. Even students who wanted to work during the summers and part-time during the school year found it rather easy to get jobs.

And, of course, there was plenty to eat. Nearly all the local families had home gardens, and many also raised chickens, rabbits and other animals for home consumption.

Furthermore, small towns were surrounded by farms, large, commercial gardens, and an abundance of farmers' markets.

Molly, her family, and all the people she knew had adequate incomes to meet their needs, even after the Wall Street Crash. Furthermore, immediately after she graduated she was able to get a job, albeit low-paying, working as a sales clerk in a grocery store in town. She'd continued to live at home, and was close enough to the store that she could walk to and from work, although she often was given a ride, by some kind young man wanting to find out if she was available the following weekend.

Sometimes she was.

Often she was already booked up.

'I'm so sorry, my dance card is full that whole weekend,' she would declare sweetly, and the boy would roll his eyes and obtain a commitment from her quickly for the next time the traveling carnival was in town.

It was Molly's turn to close up the store on the day her frivolous and fun approach to life ended. She'd carefully tallied the cash, stored it in the safe out the back away from potential robbers (although nothing so exciting ever happened in their town, she reflected occasionally), and cleared the snow from the path to make it easier to access the building in the morning - especially if it snowed again overnight.

As she turned the key in the door and rattled it to make sure it was properly closed, she heard her name being called from across the street.

It was Fred, one of the boys she was courting with from time to time. 'I've come to take you home, Molly,' he called through cupped hands.

'Fred! You know I'm not available until Wednesday after the church supper.'

Fred shook his head. 'I'm sorry, Molly, but this is something different. The sheriff just called for my father, and they told me I should get you home as quickly as possible.'

'The ... your father?'

What was going on? Fred's father was the town's doctor, and her own father often called him if there was an injury to deal with or a death to notarize. 'Has something happened at the jail?'

She was beside the car; Fred scurried around from his side and ushered her into the passenger seat, as chivalrous as ever. 'It's not the jail, Molls, it's your mother.'

Molly felt her heart being squeezed from within. 'But she's recovered, hasn't she?'

'I'm sorry, Molly. My dad thinks it's pneumonia,' said Fred. 'Very serious. He's sending her back to the hospital.'

During the exceptionally cold and snowy winter, her mother had come down with influenza. Molly's father, ever cautious, had taken her to the hospital, but after a few days she'd recovered enough to be sent home, joking that all she'd needed was the vacation.

Now, just days later, it appeared she'd had a relapse.

'Get me home as quickly as you can, Fred, please,' said Molly. 'I need to see her.'

'I'll do what I can.' Fred glanced nervously at the whitening sky. 'But I think there's a new blizzard coming in fast.'

He was right. By the time they'd driven past the school and the baseball field, the fields were indiscernible, blanketed by snow. The silver pale sky blended into the horizon so that all around them there was only a chill white fog, stretching as far as they could see.

Fred's anxiety was increasing. 'If I get you to your place, I'll never get home again.'

They were crawling along at about two miles an hour.

'We'll never even get close at this rate.' Molly scraped ineffectually at the inside of the windshield. 'I don't know what to do,' she whispered, feeling helpless for the first time in her life.

Fred shook his head again. 'Me neither. But I don't think it'll help anyone to have you in the hospital, too. Let's sit it out and see how the roads are when the storm has passed.'

'No! Fred, you're a genius.' Molly kissed his cold cheek quickly. 'If Mom was going to the hospital when you were sent to fetch me, she should have been there before the snowstorm began. Let's drive there instead.'

But the car wasn't going anywhere. Very glad of her athletic abilities, Molly wrapped her muffler firmly around her neck and set off at a run.

She arrived within twenty minutes, slithering and sliding along the corridors as she sought out the room her mother might be in. Spotting Doctor Carter in the distance, she ran full-speed to the isolation room, not caring whether it was ladylike or not.

'Doctor Carter, Fred's on his way,' she cried, clutching his sleeve.

'Thank goodness.' Fred's father's brow creased as he took in Molly's soaked shoes. 'I was worried you'd try to get all the way out to the homestead.'

'Is my mother here?'

Doctor Carter gazed at her for a moment, then nodded. He indicated the door ahead of him. 'Jesse's with her. You can go in. Just … she's really gone downhill, Molly. Be prepared.'

Her father's uniform stood out against the stark whiteness of the ward as he stood uneasily by her mother's bed. Molly rushed to his side, halted by the sight of her stricken mother. She lay beneath the blankets like a child, a bird, fragile and barely making an impression on the mattress. Molly could hear her chest rattling as she struggled to drag air into her embattled chest, but other than that there was no movement at all. It was if her mother's spirit had already left, leaving behind an empty body.

'Dad,' said Molly. 'What … why is she sleeping like that?'

Her father's eyes were sunken, almost as if he, too, was ill. 'She has a severe case of pneumonia. In her weakened state, she quickly lapsed into a coma. We're just hoping she'll improve now that she's here. She went downhill so fast, Molly. So fast. I couldn't get there in time.'

'She'll get better now, though, won't she? She's in the right place, with all this expert care and the doctors right here…'

But her father didn't answer, and somehow she knew what they all suspected, what Doctor Carter had tried to warn her to expect.

Her mother never regained consciousness, dying after only a few more days.

Molly was absolutely devastated by her mother's death. Even worse, her father was rendered despondent and nearly helpless. He didn't know which way to turn in running the household. He had never thought about being responsible for running the home, let alone doing it. He had never given a thought to life without his wife.

It took many weeks for him to learn how to function at even a basic level without the constant support and guiding light of his wife in the home, but then one evening, as Molly returned from the store, he called her into the kitchen.

'I don't know how to cope without her,' he said simply, and Molly nodded, biting her lip to prevent the tears from flowing.

'You know I'll do anything I can,' she said.

'I … I don't like to ask.' Jesse picked at the table top with a ground-down fingernail, something he'd been doing more and more over the passing weeks when he had to face something unpleasant.

'What is it, Dad?'

He sighed. 'I know you love your job, but I was wondering if you would consider quitting. Stay here in the home, and essentially take over the household. You could have room and board as part of your compensation for running the home, and I'll match your earnings from the store so that you can continue to save money for your future. I know it's a lot to ask, Molly, but I just don't … I just don't know …'

She did not hesitate to do as her father asked.

Molly immediately quit her job and began the process of learning to run the household. It took a while to get used to her mother being gone, and to get settled into a workable routine of taking care of her father, paying the bills, and running the home.

For a long while, she stopped going out on dates, but gradually she reached the point of occasionally accepting invitations to picture shows or to be escorted to community events.

Somehow, though, it was no longer enough. The fancy-free approach of old Molly no longer suited a mature young woman who had experienced great sadness and learned to run a household. How could she gad about with such frivolity? No. Her thoughts turned increasingly to marriage, to stability, and maybe even children of her own, but she couldn't bear the thought of leaving her father alone. In fact, the only men who seemed suitable to date were Jesse's deputies, who visited him at home more frequently since the death of his wife, mostly on business, but occasionally for social events such as cook-outs.

There were three deputies who paid her particular attention, all of them older than her by between two and eight years. The youngest and oldest ones were bachelors, and the 25-year-old was a divorcee.

It was clear, from the beginning, that her father was very pleased that she was finally dating men whom he not only admired, but also whom he felt would be able to adequately provide for a wife and children.

'You go ahead,' he told her when she expressed an interest in John, one of the two younger deputies. 'They're good men, all of them. And don't forget Tommy. I know he's a little reserved, but I have the feeling he likes you too.'

For her own part, she liked all three of the men she dated, especially the two youngest ones. Without exception, she always had a good time on her dates, and gradually they became increasingly romantic. She had actually begun to become hopeful that one of the younger men would propose to her, but somehow it didn't happen.

The older bachelor, Tommy, remained constant, almost vigilant in his caring attention toward her, but always seemly and never pushing her in the way the younger ones sometimes did. She began to see what Maureen had alluded to – a strong marriage like their parents', with a steady income and a gentle easy relationship, perhaps even children like Eddie and the new-born twins, Gilbert and Graham.

Eventually, her father also began to talk to her about her future. He expressed no thoughts of ever taking another wife, but instead began talking about the possibility of her getting married and raising her children somewhere special.

'If you wanted to do that, Molly, I would deed the home to you, with the proviso that I would continue to live here, and you could look after me into my old age. That's an exciting prospect, isn't it?' he added with a flash of his old, droll humour.

'It really is,' she told him.

The idea of being able to live her whole lifetime in the home that she had always loved began to intrigue her. Moreover, she had always loved her father, and, since her mother's death, they had worked well together in keeping the household running.

She gradually came to agree with her father's plan for her future. It didn't require her to marry, but it allowed for the possibility, and for both to be secure in the knowledge that they were cared for.

Jesse wrote a will that deeded her the ownership of the family home, most of its contents, and the real estate, upon his death. It also gave his other five children fair shares of his estate in the form of other properties, investment securities and money. Around six months after her mother's death, she was established as the inheritor of the family home, with an obligation to care for her father, and to run the household. In all other regards, including which men she walked out with, she was free to do as she pleased.

In time, Tommy became her most frequent escort, and the other two dropped out of the running.

'I think we'd better cool it, Molly. Not worth upsetting the boss,' said John abruptly one evening as he said goodbye.

'My father? You're not upsetting him.'

'Let's just ... leave it, okay, Molly?'

He didn't look particularly like a man who wanted to leave it, and as Arlen had said something similar, she wondered for a moment whether Jesse had warned them off for some reason. Then she saw a car's headlights turning out of the end of the drive after she'd waved a sorry farewell to John, and the small suspicion occurred to her that they might have been referring to the more senior deputy, rather than the sheriff.

The next night, her suspicions were confirmed when the older deputy reached for her fingers across the table, after a private dinner on the back porch.

'Tommy,' she said with a smile. 'Did you frighten the other two off?'

He held her hand tightly, gazing at her with his customary intensity. 'They weren't serious about you, and I am. I couldn't have you wasting your time with those boys when you and I are meant to be together,' he said, squeezing her fingers. 'Molly, I'd be extremely pleased if you would do me the honor of becoming my wife.'

Molly thought about it. It worked. They would have a marriage like her mom and dad's, and live in the family home, and she would be part of the town and family organism, just as she'd always known she would be.

And she most definitely wasn't related to him.

'Yes,' she said gently. 'Yes, I accept.'

She wasn't entirely sure that she had made the right decision, but her father was extremely pleased about it, and meanwhile the town delighted in drawing its extended family in, ever closer.

Chapter 4

The Bells are Ringing

They're congregatin' for me and my gal
While the parson's waitin' for me and my gal
And sometime I'm gonna build a little home for two, three or four or more
In love land for me and my gal

Me and My Girl, Douglas Furber and L. Arthur Rose

It was the town wedding to end all town weddings, organised by Tommy's sister, Carol, who turned out to be a dab hand at planning events, as well as an ideal sister-in-law for Molly. She was only a year younger than Molly, and full of great ideas and genuine warmth.

'We'll keep it simple,' she'd suggested. 'A real country wedding at your home, Molly, where nobody feels left out.'

The Depression was beginning to make its presence known even out in the country, where its impact hadn't been so direct, so a straightforward wedding where everyone could attend sounded perfect.

No wedding invitations were sent out. Instead, invitations were made by word-of-mouth, either directly, or by asking people to pass the word around the community. Everyone in the community was invited, along with family members and friends who lived in other nearby towns and communities.

Over two hundred people attended, with every single one of the adults bringing something to contribute to the potluck dinner reception following the wedding ceremony. Altogether, it would be a great feast: a huge array of meats, such as hams, fried chicken, roast beef, and rabbit; a variety of casseroles; many kinds of vegetable dishes; a veritable harvest of baked breads, fruit pies, cakes, and many other kinds of fruit and delicious desserts. Moreover, the attendees brought enough tables, benches and chairs to accommodate everyone for the feast, as well as for the ceremony.

As the people poured in and Carol directed set-up operations out in the garden, Molly and her bridal party were sequestered upstairs in the house, all busily getting dressed and made up for the ceremony. Finding it hard not to shed a tear, Molly dressed carefully in her mother's wedding gown, adorning it with her mother's engagement ring and wedding jewelry. Next door, Tommy would be donning a brand-new Deputy Sheriff's uniform and tucking her mother's wedding ring into his pocket, ready to place on her finger when called for during the ceremony.

When Molly and her attendants exited the house to walk to the ceremony site, they were overwhelmed to see so many people congregated around it.

'You're the luckiest bride in Christendom,' said Carol, tucking a stray hair under Molly's veil. 'All these people! You two sure are popular.'

'They really are,' said a familiar voice.

Molly was met by her father, who was wearing his formal dress uniform.

'She'd be so proud to see you, here in her gown,' he whispered as they approached the wooden arbor, beautifully festooned with flowers and ribbons.

'And you, Dad,' said Molly. 'She'd be bursting with pride for you.'

They inhaled at the same moment, drawing strength from each other for the ceremony ahead, and the changes that had already happened.

Ahead stood the Methodist minister (who was her great uncle, Albert), awaiting her arrival. Resplendent in their formal dress uniforms, Tommy and his best man, also a deputy sheriff, both looked incredibly handsome. Splendid, even.

Molly smiled at her husband-to-be. He returned her glance with his usual intense gaze, and for a moment, she longed to see passion and joy in his eyes instead of his normal serious steadfastness. But someone steadfast was wonderful. A sheriff like her father, so that she could be a home-maker like her mother. Perfectly wonderful.

'Here we go, Dad,' she said to her father.

With the bridesmaids walking ahead of her, she and Jesse passed beneath an archway formed from two rows of six deputy sheriffs each, facing each other with raised swords. It was quite a sight to see, and Molly was happy to note how the deputies were honoring her father as much as they were celebrating her nuptials with their colleague.

Soon she was standing beside Tommy, conscious of his closeness, his relative maturity. He would be thirty before too long, while she had only recently turned twenty-one. She had chosen well; she was sure of it. A decent man, ready to cherish and look after her.

The ceremony was unrehearsed, quiet, somber, and very serious, lasting about fifteen minutes. As she repeated the words of the minister, her mood changed quite perceptively from one of uncertainty to one of happy anticipation of a bright and secure future. Although she still had doubts about whether she truly loved Tommy, being uncertain what "love" actually meant or even felt like, she nevertheless took her vows seriously. She would love, honor and obey Tommy until her dying day.

When the ceremony ended with a chaste kiss from Tommy, Molly felt exquisitely happy - perhaps happier than she had ever been in her life. Excited by the whole memorable day, she joined Tommy in accepting the many blessings and congratulations during the reception, and was absolutely thrilled to join the throng in the celebratory feast.

It was a warm, sunny, day, and there were enough trees in the large yard to arrange the tables so that everyone was shaded and comfortable. During the meal, deputy sheriffs would drop in to eat at various times, as they came off duty or left to take over. The crowd was alive with people coursing about as they went to and from the food tables. Molly drank in the chatter of excited conversation and the continuous roll of laughter, punctuated occasionally with outbursts of hilarity. It was quite evident that a good time was being had by all.

From time to time, Tommy would reach out and squeeze the ends of her fingers, as he had done the night he'd proposed.

She felt almost bashful in his presence. While all this planning was taking place, she had spent very little time alone with Tommy. Even when they were alone they spent almost no time discussing either the upcoming wedding or their plans for the future.

That was, perhaps, because all plans for the future were fairly settled: Molly's father had made it quite clear that he expected Molly and her husband to live in the family home as if it was theirs. Jesse would be a roomer there, and Molly would take care of him much as she was presently doing. As Tommy was one of his Deputy Sheriffs as well as his son-in-law; they all needed to be extraordinarily careful to prevent people from thinking that Tommy was getting special treatment in the County Sheriffs' Department, but they all agreed with everything Jesse suggested, and it hadn't been necessary to talk much further. Not much further at all.

The party began to wind down perceptively as the daylight began to fade. As the crowd thinned, Molly started to become apprehensive about what would happen when she and Tommy were alone in their bedroom. Like every girl and young lady in the country, she had frequently seen animals copulate, and families and local communities routinely exposed children to the "birds and bees" and the "facts of life". As a virgin, however, she had never experienced it herself. Maureen had hinted that it was a joy, something to look forward to, but Molly still couldn't help feeling nervous about what was to come.

Finally, when the guests had all departed and her father had tactfully excused himself and gone to bed, she and Tommy entered their bedroom. She half-expected Tommy to sweep her up in his arms and kiss her with unbridled passion such as she'd seen at the movies, now that he was her husband.

Instead, he nodded to her with that strange, intense gaze.

'You can use the bathroom first,' he told her.

'Oh. Thank you. That's …' What was that? Unexpected? 'Kind,' she finished.

It was kind. He knew she was nervous. Tommy was older and had perhaps had some sexual experience before. This was his way of allaying her fears.

The clock chimed half past the hour. It was eleven thirty. It took Molly a few minutes to undress and put on the new nightgown she'd bought specially for the occasion. She slipped back into the bedroom and perched on the edge of the bed, unsure of herself. Tommy's dark eyes raced up and down her body, then he turned abruptly, holding his toothbrush, and disappeared out to the bathroom.

By the time he returned, it was close to midnight. Tommy approached her with almost military intention, grasping her by the hands to pull her to her feet. He pressed his face against hers with a ferocious intensity, but Molly felt no affection in the kiss. Where she expected to taste toothpaste and freshness, she met with the sour tang of whisky.

'Did you have a nightcap?' she asked gently. 'I can bring it to you in future.'

She would honor and obey him. And it was his wedding day – why shouldn't he celebrate with a drink?

Tommy drew back his head. 'No need,' he growled. 'I can get my own liquor.'

'I just thought—'

'Get on the bed,' he said brusquely.

Molly's breath caught in her throat. She'd hoped to climb under the covers, to be caressed gently and kissed and loved … but perhaps this was the way. Perhaps this was the way of all married couples. Honor and obey, she reminded herself.

'All right, I'll—'

She hadn't even begun to lie down when, suddenly, all hell broke loose. Beyond the bedroom walls, out in the yard where just an hour ago they had danced to gentle music, it sounded as if a war had erupted. Bells clanged and guns were going off as a chorus of men's voices began shouting and calling. Above their heads, a criss-cross of flashlight beams played on the ceiling and walls of the bedroom. The window being open on such a warm night made the din that much louder. It was bedlam.

'Tommy, what is it?' cried Molly, gathering her nightgown around her as if it could protect her.

'Those bastards.' Tommy jumped out of bed and ran to the window. 'Hey, you lousy, noisy bastards! I'm trying to screw my wife in here!'

That was all the provocation they needed, apparently. Raucous laughter and filth such as Molly had never heard before rang out across the yard as Tommy shouted out of the window, gun-shots raining all around them so that Molly feared for her life.

'Stay here; I'll be back in a few minutes,' yelled Tommy.

Molly grabbed his arm. 'Don't go out there! You'll get hurt.'

'You don't know what you're talking about,' said Tommy, shaking off Molly's hand. 'Those are my friends out there.'

'But it's our wedding night.'

He held up his hands as if she was talking nonsense. 'That's why they're here,' he snorted.

Then, still shouting obscenities through the window, Tommy pulled on his shorts, grabbed his robe, and ran out of the room. Molly stayed in bed and listened. In a few minutes the shooting and bell ringing died down, but the laughter and shouting continued. She crept to the window, being sure not to cast a shadow. Every now and then she could hear Tommy speaking and laughing, and she thought that she also recognized his best man's deep voice. Her own name and Tommy's were frequently mentioned, and then she heard the clink of bottles, the tiny glug of liquor being poured.

Alone and scared, Molly slid down the wall until she crouched on the floor, wondering what was happening while the loud cursing, the obscene language and the laughter ebbed and flowed and eventually died down, to be replaced by the deep murmurs of just a few people.

It was over an hour before she began to hear the slamming of truck and car doors, followed by the sound of Tommy clomping up the stairs to their room.

He opened the door and, rather unsteadily, reeled to his side of the bed as he threw his robe and shorts to the floor.

'It was a belling.' He reeked of whiskey and was slurring his words. 'Just my ... my friends with a belling.'

She had heard of these loud, boisterous and often drunken gatherings of men beneath the windows of just-married couples, but the actual experience of being subjected to one was much worse than she could ever have imagined.

'A traditional belling, for the bridegroom,' he slurred. 'The happy, happy bridegroom.'

'Aren't you happy, Tommy?' He didn't sound as if he was happy. More like he was angry.

He didn't reply. Instead, very roughly, he shoved her back onto the bed, hoisted up her nightgown and took her in one or two painful thrusts that felt as though they were ripping her apart - much, she thought, as a bull would take a cow. He grunted once, breathing whiskey fumes into her face as his seed trickled down her thigh, mingled with the slick of blood. Then he then rolled off her and almost immediately began to snore like a freight train.

Molly was mortified that her wedding night – no worse, her wedding bed - would end up being so horrible. Shivering, she crept to the bathroom and cleaned herself up. Then she slid beneath the bedclothes beside the sprawled-out figure of her husband, and waited silently for dawn to come.

She didn't have the opportunity to talk about the belling the next morning with Tommy or her father, because they left for work immediately after wolfing down a quick breakfast. After they left, she busied herself around the house, all the time thinking about what might happen in bed that night. She had a very nice dinner ready shortly after her father and Tommy arrived from work. As they ate, her father and Tommy talked about sheriffing events of the day, but most of the discussion was about the wedding and, especially, the feast.

Then it was time to go to bed and to face her second sexual encounter with her new husband.

She was very apprehensive - even more than she had been on her wedding night.

Her fears turned out to be justified. After getting into bed, they lay in silence for a while. Then in a sudden movement Tommy rolled on top of her, humped and sweated on her for several minutes, and then rolled off her to quickly fall asleep.

It was a terrible and painful experience, much worse than the night before. There was no caressing, no love talk, no gentleness ... only Tommy's grunting and groaning, followed by his obnoxious snoring.

Chapter 5

The Prisoner

*Real courage is when you're licked before you begin,
But you begin anyway and see it through no matter what.*

To Kill a Mockingbird, Harper Lee

Immediately after the trial, Charlie was transported from the jail to the State Penitentiary, to spend the rest of his life in prison.

It took several days to be processed into the prison, and several more days to be integrated to prison life and prison routine. On the first day, he was assigned to a cell, where at first he was the sole occupant. After a physical examination by the prison doctor, he was issued with clothing, shoes, bedding, toiletries and a stack of papers. These included prison rules, regulations and procedures and the penalties and punishments for breaking them; descriptions of prison facilities, and opportunities for employment, education, recreation and hobbies.

He spent the first night lying on an unmade bed, staring at the white-washed wall and wondering, over and over and over, how he had come to be here.

On the second day, he met with the warden.

'You're our youngest inmate,' Warden Kelly informed him. 'That could make life difficult for you in here. Yes,' he said in response to the obvious question on Charlie's face, 'even more difficult than having to spend the rest of your days in incarceration. Plenty of older guys in here might see you as sport. Fair game. And of course, there's nothing fair about it.'

The warden circled the table and perched on the edge nearest Charlie, looking at him in pretty much the same way that Mr Adams had regarded him – sadly, as if he'd seen too much of life and didn't want to expose a youngster to it all at once.

After a while he let out a sigh.

'You see, Charlie,' he said gently, rifling through the sheaf of papers that Charlie had needed to sign, 'there are two ways to consider your life in prison. On the one hand, you can see it as pure punishment for the wrongdoing you perpetrated, and if that's what you feel, then every day will be a living hell for you, young man. A living hell, for the rest of your life.'

Charlie nodded, understanding completely. He was a good Catholic boy; he'd known about Hell since he was tiny. 'What's ... what's on the other hand, sir?'

'I'm glad you asked.' Warden Kelly smiled approvingly. 'On the other hand ... you can see this as a chance to improve yourself. There's nothing to say your education must stop, or your learning. You're an intelligent young man, despite your obvious lapse in judgment. I would encourage you to make the best of your imprisonment by taking advantage of the many opportunities offered by the prison.

I'm really quite proud of our facilities, and I'd be even more pleased if someone were to make the very best of them.'

The warden then introduced him to three counselors who would be available to help make his life in prison as personally rewarding and enjoyable as he could possibly want. The quality of his prison life and the number of achievements would be strictly up to him.

He left the warden's office with a good feeling. Before he was dragged out of the get-away car at the bank, he had never given a thought to what prison life might be like. Why would he? However, after that, and until his meeting with the warden, he had imagined that prison life was horrible, dangerous and degrading. Now he was feeling very upbeat and optimistic that prison life might not be so bad after all. It might even be enjoyable and rewarding.

It was strictly up to him, and he intended to consider it a miracle rather than a curse.

Like Mr Adams had told him, he'd avoided the chair, and he was going to spend every day of the rest of his life ... yes, in prison, but also thanking the good Lord for sparing him at this young age. As he was led back to his solo cell, Charlie determined to count his blessings in every way possible.

Feeling less overwhelmed and depressed, Charlie straightened up as the prison guard led him past the other prisoners to his cell. For the first time, he felt able to look around. He passed the cell beside his own, number 248, and slowed to see his neighbor. To his astonishment, he found himself looking into the prominent eyes of a man with skin as black as coal.

The guard pushed him forward. 'Doesn't do to stare in prison, boy.'

The eyes behind the rails dimmed immediately as the black man dropped his gaze down to the floor.

Charlie swallowed. 'I never saw a colored man before,' he said softly.

'Ain't never robbed a bank before, neither, right? It sure is a time of new experiences for you, boy. Just don't have any more on my watch, okay?'

The guard was opening the door to his cell with his enormous chain of keys. He waited for Charlie to walk past him and clanged the door closed behind him.

Charlie hesitated, then turned around.

'Sir?'

The guard's face re-appeared in the small aperture that opened, Charlie thought, like his mother's cuckoo clock.

'I just want to say that I didn't rob the bank, sir,' said Charlie. 'But I know it looks like I did, and I'm going to make sure I spend every day remembering that fact and trying to make amends for it. I won't make any trouble, not on your watch nor anyone else's.'

The guard raised one eyebrow. 'Is that so? Well, in that case, we'll get along fine.'

'I hope so, sir.' Charlie sucked in a breath, before blurting out: 'Also, I would very much like to know the name of my neighbor so that I can introduce myself.'

'His name is Two Four Eight,' said the guard.

'I ... I would like to know his actual name, sir, if I may?'

'I'm not entirely sure I know it,' said the guard, scratching his head, 'or that you should either. Folks keep themselves to themselves in here, boy.'

But suddenly a deep voice rang out from the small cell beside him. 'Amos,' said the young man. 'My name is Amos. And your name is Boy, right?'

Charlie laughed. 'No, sir. My name is Charlie. It's a pleasure to meet with you, Amos.'

Still shaking his head, the guard closed the cuckoo-clock door. 'No more talking, d'ye hear?' he called from the other side of the metal. 'You're not in here to cosy up and make friends.'

But Charlie thought that it was possible he was here to do precisely that. Learn, and help, and make some friends. It would be an unusual life, for sure.

But at least it would be a life.

After a few weeks in which he did manage to get to know Amos at least a little (he'd been caught stealing groceries from a township about seventy miles away, where the Depression had really taken a hold), Charlie was moved to a permanent two-man cell, which was already occupied by another lifer. Justin was twenty years his senior and had already been in prison for more than ten years. He had been told by one of the counselors that Justin was a model prisoner, exceptionally active, and the kind of man whom all the other prisoners looked up to and respected.

Charlie liked Justin right away, and asked his advice and recommendations on everything he did. Over the many years to come, their relationship was to become one of father and son, which was just as well, given that his own father had disowned him. In fact, in the thirteen years between Charlie's initial incarceration and his father's death, his father never once visited him and he had absolutely no communication with his father, either directly nor indirectly.

He had been in prison for approximately one year when he experienced a dramatic reminder of how lucky he was in not having been executed for his crime. Hepworth, who had been injured in the robbery, died in the hospital. Had he survived, of course, he would have been executed. According to many of Charlie's fellow prisoners, the gang leader had "cheated" the electric chair.

Charlie had very few visitors during his first few years at the penitentiary, but he tried not to let it bother him very much. Instead, he kept busy. There was so much for him to do there. He was taking high school courses, trade school courses, spending time in the library and in the prison's recreational facilities, and spending a lot of time talking to Justin on a myriad of subjects when he was back in his cell, or to Amos when he was in the prison's libraries. He also worked in the wood-working, metal and print shops, for employment as well as for trade school instruction. Not only was he keeping very busy, but he was also learning a lot and even enjoying himself.

Although he was allowed visitors every weekend, he seldom had more than a visitor a month. His most frequent visitors during those early years were his oldest brother, William, and one of his paternal aunts, Edna. His mother finally visited him during the third year, and then came occasionally after that - mostly on holidays. He found out that her visits were less frequent than she wanted them to be, because of his father. His father never got over the hurt, outrage, and embarrassment of the humiliation his crime had caused the family. To keep the peace, his mother had to be very careful not to antagonize her husband.

He was very understanding and accepting of his father's attitude, and never pressured his mother to visit him. Nevertheless, he especially enjoyed her visits, and always became nostalgic about her unconditional love and guidance, and the wonderful aromas of fresh-baked breads and biscuits which had always permeated their home. She began to come more frequently after her husband died, but by then she became severely invalided and was unable to travel without assistance.

His life trickled on. By the time he was twenty years old, Charlie had taken every high school level and trade school course which were available to him, and even though Amos was older, he'd persuaded him to do the same alongside him.

'You know what I'm going to do?' Charlie asked Amos one afternoon when they were re-stacking the shelves with returned books.

'Run for president?' Amos laughed with his customary good humor. Nothing ever seemed to rattle him, even when his young children visited him in prison and left in tears. 'You could be the first lifer to lead the country.'

Charlie pretended to consider it, then laughed. 'Nope. Not yet, anyways. No, what I'm going to do is read every single book in this library.'

Amos studied the spine of the book he was holding and located its position on the shelf. He'd been able to read when he entered prison but not much; Charlie's friendship and tutelage had pushed him to higher levels in all sorts of ways, especially in mental arithmetic, for which he had a natural talent. 'You're even going to read this one?'

He held up a copy of Gone With the Wind.

'Even that one.' Charlie winced at the thought, but a promise – even to himself – was a promise.

'Actually, I asked Mr Danvers about getting hold of some more mathematical books,' said Amos thoughtfully, 'and he said we could borrow books from the public libraries outside of the prison.'

'Really?' That was amazing. 'You might just have saved me from some very long tales of passion, Amos. Now I can really target what I'd like to read.'

'You and me both, Charlie. You and me both.'

Truth be told, he didn't have much time for tales of passion in any case. His close association with the church, including the legacy of his scripture lessons with Father Patton, had helped Charlie to control his sexual desires whenever he had them. He'd been an altar boy, for goodness' sake; he'd even been considering the priesthood.

Whenever such thoughts would enter his mind, which they often did during visitation periods which exposed him to women from the outside, he simply thought of the celibacy such a life would have required. His prison counsellors included the priest, Father Hannity, and Sister Brighid, who were also very effective in helping him to overcome sexual desires, particularly at times when they began to overwhelm him because of something Amos or Justin said about their wives.

Or when he saw Muriel, the young daughter of Cecil, one of the other lifers.

'Celibacy. Celibacy,' he would repeat to himself, and somehow it worked.

All in all, Charlie was comfortable with his lot. He knew he was in prison for life, for something he'd never intended to do or known would create such harm, but he spent every day doing just as Mr Adams and Warden Kelly had told him: counting his blessings, reading his Bible, learning both trades and academic subjects alike. His friendships were deep-seated and rewarding, and he had enough visitors to keep in touch with the outside world.

And then the outside world stepped into the prison.

Pearl Harbor dramatically changed everything at the Penitentiary.

It was Amos who told him about it, running into the woodwork shop where Charlie was fashioning a toy figurine for William's son.

'We can volunteer, Charlie! We can get out of here!' Amos waved a poster in Charlie's face. 'There's not enough manpower in the services, especially after Pearl Harbor with America joining in the war completely. The Government's agreed that prisoners who volunteer for the armed forces can have their sentences commuted or be granted parole early.'

'Oh, my Lord, Amos. That's our way out. That's our way out!'

Clutching each other's arms, they bounced up and down among the woodwork benches, hearing the cheers as the news spread around the prison.

'What do we do? How do we volunteer?' said Amos breathlessly.

Charlie knew instantly. 'I'm going to straight to the Warden. And you're coming with me.'

They joined the queue that had formed at the Warden's office door, made up mostly of younger men like themselves. The guards shepherded them half-heartedly along the corridor, clearly wondering how much easier their life was going to be with all the young bloods fighting for their country. Maybe they were even thinking of signing up themselves.

Charlie pushed Amos through the Warden's door first and waited until he emerged, grinning, before allowing himself a little rush of anticipation. He hadn't been looking for a way out of prison, of course, but if there was a route that allowed him to be paroled and to serve his country, then he wanted to be one of the first to volunteer.

Finally, he stood before the warden's desk, only realizing then that he was still clutching the half-chiselled figurine. He shoved it behind him.

'Warden Kelly, sir, I'd like to volunteer to serve in the armed forces.'

Kelly stared at him bleakly, and Charlie faltered a little.

'I ... I'm in excellent physical condition, sir. I have numerous skills both from my time in the penitentiary and my life on the farm before I came here, especially with engines. I believe I could help out a lot with planes and service vehicles, Warden Kelly. I'm also exceptionally well-educated, all thanks to the many opportunities that I've taken here in prison, sir. Just like you said I should. I—'

He stopped short, because the Warden wasn't responding. He looked pained, with that sad, wearied expression clouding his eyes once more.

'I'm sorry, son,' he said eventually. 'I don't disagree with a single thing you've just said. If it was up to me, I'd say you were the best qualified volunteer of all. The most likely to do his country proud. A young man in the prime of life. But it's out of my hands, I'm afraid.'

'What do you mean, sir?'

The warden picked up a circular from his desk, and read it aloud. 'We are not allowing early release of any prisoners who are serving a life sentence, particularly if their crimes involved murder and especially the murder of law-enforcement officers, regardless of the amount of time already served and irrespective of how good their prison records are.' Kelly shook his head regretfully. 'I'm afraid that means you, Charlie.'

'But Warden Kelly, there must be something you can do.'

Again, the man shook his head. 'I can't fight the Federal Government – even when I think they're wrong.'

And that was how it was to be. Amos left within a few days, along with several of the younger inmates. They shook hands warmly, and promised to write whatever happened to Amos and wherever he may find himself – because Charlie was going nowhere. From then until the end of the war, every time a call went out for volunteers from the prisons, he put himself forward - to no avail.

This became a source of great frustration to him, because all six of his brothers, two brothers-in-law, and many of his fellow prisoners were serving in the various theaters of war. His next youngest brother, who was already in the service when the war started, was serving with Patton in North Africa and Europe; his three oldest brothers volunteered in early 1942, with two serving with the Marines in the South Pacific (where Amos had found himself too) and the other serving with the Army in the European theater. His two youngest brothers volunteered toward the end of the war, after they turned eighteen, and joined the Army in the North Pacific.

He followed the war as closely as he could, especially the units in which his brothers, including Amos, served. He requested that his brothers correspond with him as often as they could, and four of them did. He did his part, sending post cards and letters often to all six - even to the two who did not write back. He would forever be disappointed that the authorities would not allow him to serve in the armed forces. He always thought that if he had been given the opportunity he would have volunteered for the Marine Corps, like his oldest brother, William, whom he admired and respected most of all.

During the war, William's wife, Marie, and their three children became his most frequent visitors. These were the only times that he was visited by children, and he very much enjoyed being with his nephew, Russell, and two nieces. Most of time his sister-in-law brought all three children with her, but sometimes she came with only Russell. On nearly every visit, he gave the children wooden toys that he or his fellow inmates had created in the wood shop.

On one of these visits, Russel broke away from their table and ran over to Muriel.

'You're pretty!' he cried bluntly, in the way only a child can, and everyone around them laughed.

For the first time, Charlie caught Muriel's eyes. She flushed scarlet, though whether it was because of what Russel had said or because she had noticed Charlie looking at her, he couldn't be sure.

When Cecil had first introduced his family to him, Muriel was sixteen years old, and Charlie was thirty-three. He had already been in prison for eighteen years, and had met Cecil when he first began to work in the prison print shop after requesting that he be given the opportunity to learn the printing trade. When added to his previous experiences in the metal-working and wood-working shops, this would give him expertise in three trades.

He was well-educated, well-rounded, and highly skilled – but a complete novice when it came to affairs of the heart. As he saw Muriel blush, he felt his own skin grow hot, and he quickly called for Russell to stop bothering Cecil and his family. His nephew had broken the ice, at least. From now on he and Muriel could chat together as adults, even if it could never go any further than friendship.

Apart from anything else, it was pointless to hope. Despite all his volunteering, he was never getting out of prison. Even when Justin, along with two of his counselors and several other prisoners, began to talk of the possibility that some Lifers might be eligible for parole after serving only 20 years, Charlie reasoned that the State legislature was always considering such bills and they always fell short of the votes needed to pass, besides the fact that those sentenced to life without parole would generally not be eligible.

Nonetheless, Charlie allowed himself to dream - just a little - of a life with Muriel, and how wonderful it would be. He could visualize himself and Muriel, living on a little farm with a big house, permeated with the wonderful aroma of baked biscuits and breads as his own home had been and, most importantly filled with happy little children - his children!

While all the hubbub about early releases was filtering through the prison, the Korean War broke out. Again, prisoners were getting early releases to supplement the selective service draft. Charlie was again among the earliest in his penitentiary to volunteer, specifically applying for the Marine Corps or the Army Infantry, but again he was turned down.

'I have to accept it,' he told Justin. 'The new rules just don't apply to me. I'm going to die right here in this prison. Probably on this very bed.'

'Well, don't expect me to clear up your mess,' said Justin with a wry grin.

'You'll be long gone by then, old man.'

'You'll have to clear up my mess, then.'

And they'd laughed, because they knew that the other man would always be there for them, to clear up whatever mess there was, until the day one of them could do it no longer.

Finally, one day the Warden called him into his office.

'I've seen a lot of you across this desk over the years,' said Kelly with a twitch of his lips. 'No single prisoner has volunteered for service so often, and I haven't had to disappoint anyone else half as much.'

Charlie smiled. 'You don't need to do it again, Warden Kelly, sir. I've already accepted that the new parole rules won't apply to me.'

'Actually,' said Kelly deliberately, 'they might.'

'What? I mean, I beg your pardon, sir?'

'There have been changes in state law to make Lifers eligible for parole consideration, as soon as they've served at least twenty years of their sentences. Furthermore, because you were only fifteen when you began serving your sentence, you might – *might* - be eligible right away, even though you've only served a little over nineteen years.'

Charlie's heart sped up, and he clutched at the edge of the desk before he stumbled.

The Warden pushed him gently onto a chair. 'Because of your exemplary record and comparatively young age, I am going to recommend that the Parole Board waive the twenty-year requirement. We'll see if you can't be the first Lifer released under the new law.'

Charlie's eyes filled with tears. 'I don't know what to say,' he mumbled.

'Well, let's not get ahead of ourselves, but I think you have cause to be optimistic.'

'Thank you, sir.' Charlie climbed uncertainly to his feet, turned to leave the room, then spun around and reached for the warden's hand. 'Thank you, sir, so much. Even if it doesn't happen, it means so much that you're prepared to vouch for me in this way.'

'Always was, Charlie. I always was.'

He was very excited, but also very apprehensive. After not being outside the prison walls for nearly twenty years, he had a hard time visualizing himself as a civilian – perhaps even a married man, being with a woman for the first time in his life.

That weekend, he got a visitor. It was Muriel, coming to see him on her own, as if they were already sweethearts. She was still only eighteen, and in her senior year of high school, but Charlie could see only her love of life and her total acceptance of him as a human being rather than a lifer in prison.

'I ... I might be getting out,' he told her under his breath, hardly daring to speak the words in case he jinxed them.

'Charlie, oh! That's magnificent.' Muriel's hand stretched across the table, their fingertips touching.

Emboldened, Charlie held onto her left hand. 'Muriel, I know we don't know each other well, and that you're younger than me, and I'm a prisoner, and ...'

'Can you think of any more problems?' giggled Muriel.

Charlie shook his head. 'No. I can only think that I love you, and that you might love me, and that if I do get out of here soon, nothing would make me happier than to call you my wife.'

'Is ... is that a proposal, Charlie?'

'Yes!' Charlie dropped to his knee, right there in the visitor's room for all to see. 'Muriel, will you marry me?'

'Yes, Charlie, I will.'

All of a sudden, his desire for this exceptionally beautiful young lady was overwhelming. He retired that night in a state of euphoria, and even though he had a hard time falling asleep, when he did, he had the sweetest dreams of his life. Still, he remained on tenterhooks, fearing that everything that was happening was no more than those sweet dreams, and that his release would be denied by the Parole Board.

As it turned out, however, at the next meeting of the Parole Board, his release was approved.

And so it was that, nineteen years and ten months after Charlie was incarcerated, the "miracle" happened. He was released from a life sentence in the prison, to begin a new life as a civilian. He would have a beautiful wife to share that life with, and, because of his outstanding skill-set, an excellent job at the large manufacturing plant in the city which made metal tools and machinery parts. He and Muriel set their wedding date for the weekend following her graduation from high school – the week after his own graduation, from life in the state penitentiary.

Chapter 6

A Man on the Outside

Instead of getting the house like Mount Vernon, they had moved into the little house on Greentree Avenue in Westport, and Betsy had become pregnant, and he had thrown the vase against the wall, and the washing machine had broken down.

The Man in the Gray Flannel Suit, Sloan Wilson

Charlie awoke early in the morning, quickly washed up, combed his hair, and dressed carefully in the new "civilian" clothing which Muriel had brought to him two days earlier. Everything fit reasonably well: undershorts, dark socks, crisp white shirt, shiny black shoes, a nice blue-and-gray striped tie, and a medium blue, pin-striped suit which coordinated with the color of his eyes. He was both surprised and quite pleased with his image, even though he did not know how to knot his tie. He was forced to leave it draped around his neck, awaiting someone who knew how to assemble it for him.

Almost as soon as he had finished, a guard came in to escort him to the Warden's office. It was the same guard who had led him to his cell all those years ago, past Amos and the other inmates.

'So, Two Four Nine. Your day has finally come.'

Charlie's grin reached from ear-to-ear. 'I haven't been Two Four Nine since the first few weeks I was here. How did you remember that?'

'You were easy to recollect ... Charlie.' It was the first time he'd ever called him by his Christian name. 'Just a kid, and yet so determined to be good. Me and the other guards – well, we always took a little extra care to look out for you. We're all so happy that you're being paroled.'

'Finally getting rid of me, huh?'

'Exactly,' said the guard with a wink, then he opened the door to the warden's office as he had done so many times before.

Warden Kelly rose as they entered his office. 'Do you know what, young man? I think we can do better than sit around this table yet again. Why don't you both walk with me to the staff cafeteria for breakfast.'

'And I don't have to serve it?' joked Charlie.

'Not this time,' said Kelly. 'Son,' he added.

Several tables had been put together to accommodate the group which was joining them for the farewell breakfast, which included Sister Brighid, Justin, Cecil, Father Hannity, four other guards, and six other prison employees.

Before sitting down, Charlie went around the table to shake hands or hug all of them. As they enjoyed a very delicious breakfast, conversation centered around Charlie's impending marriage, his new job (he told them that, of his two offers, one in a printing firm and one in engineering, he was leaning toward working in the manufacturing plant) and most of all his relationships with those sitting around the table over the past two decades. Charlie felt as though he should probably try to rush through it, to speed up his exit, but instead he wanted to savor every last moment with these people who had so affected his life.

Before too long, however, Warden Kelly announced that he was ready to escort Charlie to the prison's processing center, where he would begin the routine of departing the prison. As he left, Charlie again made the round of hand clasps and embraces, telling them all that he would visit with them from time to time in the future.

Sister Brighid held his hands between her own. 'I'm coming with you and the Warden, Charlie,' she said tearfully, 'and I'll stay with you through the entire out-processing procedure.'

She escorted him to the exit door, where they were met by Warden Kelly brandishing an envelope.

'This contains a letter of recommendation and a list of references.' He shook Charlie's hand even more firmly than earlier. 'It's been a pleasure to have known and worked with you, young man. I consider my success in helping you get your parole approved to be the greatest accomplishment of my life.'

As the warden opened the door, Charlie said a final goodbye to Sister Brighid, who gave him a warm hug.

Finally, he stepped out of the prison for the first time in nearly twenty years. Every cell in his body seemed to be shaking, and for a moment he had to stand stock still, gathering himself together.

Then he walked forward.

Waiting to greet him were Muriel, Muriel's mother and brother, and his favorite aunt. The five of them got into Muriel's mother's car, and Aunt Edna announced that she was treating them all to a meal at her favorite restaurant to celebrate his release.

On the way to the restaurant, Charlie opened the envelope Warden Kelly had given him, to discover a four-page letter describing his activities and accomplishments during his confinement, as well as endorsements from Father Hannity, Sister Brighid, four of his other teachers and instructors, three guards, and four other prison officials. He passed the letter to Muriel who read it and, in turn, passed it around to the others.

'How does it all look to you, Charlie?' cried his aunt, fairly giddy with the joy of being able to take her favorite nephew out for lunch for the first time since he was a teenager.

Charlie was amazed by the sights he was seeing on the way to the restaurant. He couldn't believe the changes which had taken place over the past 20 years. 'It's ... it's like a completely different world to what I remember. The automobiles, the buses, the street cars. Good Lord, even the way the people are dressed. I'm going to have to learn how to knot my own tie! The streets, the buildings and storefronts, everything ... it's all so different. Was it really only twenty years I was in there?'

They all laughed, but then Muriel's brother reminded them of how much had changed. 'The world is a whole lot different now, brother. There's been a war all over the globe, remember? You kind of missed it.'

'Not for lack of trying,' said Charlie, and they all laughed again.

What Roger had said was true, though. This was a different world, a totally new home for Charlie. It was thrilling, as well as daunting, and he was gradually becoming excited about taking his place in the outside world, hopefully as a family man and a productive member of society. He stared out of the window as the strange new landscape rushed by, holding onto Muriel's hand as if it were a life-line.

As scheduled, Charlie and Muriel were married the Saturday following his release from prison. Because Charlie was Catholic, and Muriel and her family had no church affiliation, they agreed to have Father Hannity perform the wedding ceremony in the Catholic church near Muriel's mother's home. Attending the ceremony were six members of Muriel's family, six of her friends, and nine officials from the prison, not counting Father Hannity, including Sister Brighid, Warden Kelly, and seven others. Warden Kelly's wife also attended. Except for Aunt Edna, none of Charlie's relatives agreed to come.

Muriel was beautifully dressed in her grandmother's wedding gown, while Charlie wore the same suit of clothes he'd sported on the day of his release. They were a handsome couple, indeed. After the ceremony, Father Hannity gave a little speech, in which he lauded Charlie as being a victim of circumstances who had been redeemed by maintaining his strong Catholic faith, and in keeping a close relationship with the church.

'I believe God has rewarded you by arranging for you to meet and fall in love with this wonderful girl. I wish the newly-weds a long, happy and fruitful life together.'

The sentiment was shared all around the room, and the couple embarked on married life in the full knowledge and confidence that their union was somehow blessed.

The couple had accepted Muriel's mother's invitation to live with her for as long as they needed to. They agreed to stay with her until they could get a place of their own, paying half the rent and utility bills.

It was a small, two-story house, only about 1200 square feet, so it would be somewhat cramped, but they would be more than happy to make do. Upstairs, there were two bedrooms, separated by a hallway, which led to the bathroom. Downstairs, there was a modest kitchen/dining room, a small living room, and a little utility room. A door off the kitchen led down to a neat basement which contained a large coal-fueled furnace, a coal bin, and two walls of shelves which were loaded with home-canned vegetables and fruit.

The family arranged itself so that Charlie and Muriel occupied one of the upstairs bedrooms and Roger the other. Muriel's mother, Betty, would use the living room as her bedroom. They replaced the living room sofa with a convertible sofa-bed, which allowed the room to serve a dual-purpose, and for the time-being, it was a workable arrangement.

Charlie's job didn't start for a week – an intentional delay to give him time to adjust to "civilian" life.

It also allowed time for him and Muriel to adjust to being husband and wife. They were not going away, but this week-long period, in which they would be constantly together, would serve as their honeymoon. More than most newlyweds, they needed time to get used to each other, given the seventeen-year difference in their ages – and the fact that they were both virgins.

'Are you scared, honey?' asked Charlie gently as he viewed his bride, her hair fanned out on the pillow.

Muriel smiled. 'Not at all. How could I be scared of the sweetest man on earth?'

'Well, I'm a little nervous myself,' said Charlie, reaching across the bed to take her hand.

She pulled him toward the milky skin of her shoulder. 'Don't be,' she said.

And as it turned out, neither of them needed to be apprehensive or nervous on their first night in bed together. They took to each other easily and comfortably, so much so that before morning they had made love a total of four times, with only a few cat naps in between.

Leaving the bed for breakfast that morning, they both felt exceedingly happy and contented, knowing without a shadow of doubt that they were meant for each other. They were happily married. For the entire week, until Charlie had to start working at the factory, they could not get enough of each other. Each night, they made love multiple times; during the days, it seemed that they took every opportunity to reach for each other for stolen, passionate kisses, before Roger or Betty could interrupt them. During that honeymoon week, they probably made love at least two-dozen times.

The Monday after the honeymoon week, Charlie went to work. He was assigned one or more different jobs each day during his first week, starting with operating a metal lathe. Other types of equipment he operated that week were a drill press, three different punch presses, and a very complex milling machine. He'd experienced each of these machines at the prison, although the milling device there was simpler and much easier to operate. It didn't take him long to master it, however, and he remembered what a natural he was with machinery.

By the beginning of the second week, he was assigned to the milling machine, which he operated most days for the next two years. He liked the job, and very much enjoyed working at the factory.

At home, Muriel was staying busy keeping house or reading romance and detective magazines, while Betty was away working at her job as a waitress at a nearby restaurant. Muriel and Charlie had discussed the possibility of her working, perhaps also as a waitress at a restaurant. Charlie didn't mind at all if she did, at least until they had children. Before long, Betty helped Muriel get a job at the restaurant where she worked. At first, she only worked part-time, but within a few weeks she was working full time.

'Can you believe it, Charlie?' Muriel had come home from her shift at the restaurant, proudly holding her first brown envelope full of wages and tips. 'Two incomes! We've only been married a short time, and already we have so much money coming in.'

'We'd better use it wisely, then, as Amos would say,' said Charlie. 'Do you remember Amos? He was a whizz with numbers and money matters. It was only because of the Depression that he was forced to take to stealing.'

Muriel put her envelope down on the table between them and pushed it toward Charlie. 'What would Amos suggest we do, then?'

Charlie thought for a moment, then smiled. 'He'd say that we should pay our way first, and save the rest for best,' he said firmly. 'And that's exactly what we'll do. How about we use your income to pay rent to your mom, and then mine can go into a bank account to save toward buying a house?'

'Our own home, Charlie!' Muriel was so excitable sometimes, it was as if she was a girl playing with a doll's house.

'And a bank account,' said Charlie solemnly. 'Who would ever have thought?'

He tried not to think about what had happened all those years ago. It was like a ghost had taken part, not him. But walking into a bank would always make him feel a little strange.

His wife, however, was simply impressed that they'd have enough money to build their savings.

'We are quite the grown-ups,' quipped Muriel, before dragging him into the utility room for some furtive love-making.

So that was the pattern they established. During a typical week, Charlie operated machinery at the factory and Muriel and Betty worked all day at the restaurant. Muriel and Betty usually brought home food from the restaurant for their supper. They went to bed early, and arose early in the mornings. The newly-weds, of course, made love at least once, often twice, each night that they could. On Friday nights and Saturday afternoons, Muriel usually joined Betty for a few games of bingo at the Catholic church. Betty was a bingo addict, and had hardly missed a game over the past few years.

Charlie didn't like gambling, so he never went with them. Instead he would usually take in a picture show on Friday evenings, and on Saturdays he would walk about the downtown area, marvelling at all the changes which had taken place while he was in prison.

Predictably, after four months of marriage, Muriel announced that she was pregnant. She and Charlie continued their love making pace for another two months then gradually slowed to zero during the ninth month, when they welcomed into the world their daughter, Bernadette, whom they nick-named Detty. By mutual agreement, they decided that Muriel should quit her job by the seventh month of her pregnancy, and that she would stay home until their children were raised.

In compensation for the lost income, Charlie successfully volunteered for as much over-time work he could get. Moreover, at the end of one year, Charlie was rewarded with a nice raise for his excellent work performance. As a result, he was able to continue putting a substantial part of his pay check into savings while also paying their living expenses.

At the invitation of a co-worker he befriended at the factory, Charlie had also taken up fishing. His friend, Johnny, had a cabin and a fishing boat on a lake, which was stocked with game fish. Charlie quickly became an avid fisherman, and fished with Johnny as often as possible - usually a couple of weekends a month, sometimes making the excursions on Saturday mornings; staying overnight in the cabin; and returning home early Sunday afternoons, bringing home enough fish for several meals during the week.

Muriel turned out to be a good mother to Detty, and Charlie a very good father. He doted on his daughter and spent substantial parts of most evenings helping Muriel take care of her. Mostly, he played with Detty, despite the mocking he received at work for not being manly and a disciplinarian. Moreover, when Muriel and Betty played bingo, Charlie would take care of little Detty. Between the three adults and one teenager, living in the house, there was never a need to hire a babysitter. Whenever Charlie and Muriel went out on the town, usually to see a picture show, either Betty or Roger would take care of the baby.

Several times during his first year of marriage, Charlie also visited the prison to see Sister Brighid, Father Hannity, Warden Kelly, and a few of the guards who happened to be available. The only prisoner he visited, often with Muriel and Detty, was Cecil, as Justin had recently died. Most of the other inmates who had been there with Charlie had been paroled or sent off to war, so he didn't really miss any of them – apart from Amos.

The last he'd heard of Amos, he'd been in the South Pacific fending off Japs. Not for the first time, he wondered how his friend had fared during the war, and what he was doing now. The memories of prison life, however, were already beginning to fade. Maybe Charlie would just have to accept that his friendship with Amos had faded too.

Besides, there were more than enough people in his life now to keep him occupied.

More than enough.

Chapter 7

Baby Blues

When a man is wrestling a leopard in the middle of a pond,
he's in no position to run.

David Huxley in Bringing Up Baby

Early in their second year of marriage, Muriel announced that she was pregnant again.

'But Detty's only seven months old!' cried Charlie, bemused.

Muriel laughed. 'You know what we're like, Charlie. It's a wonder I wasn't pregnant again when Detty was only one month old!'

'You ... you weren't, were you?'

She didn't look that big, but Charlie wasn't sure he knew as much as he should about such matters.

'No. But the doctor said I'm probably three months pregnant.'

Charlie stared at her burgeoning belly, trying to calculate the birthdate. 'But they'll be barely a year apart. Thirteen months between Detty and the new baby!'

Muriel gave him her mischievous smile again. 'Babies. The doc's pretty sure it's twins.'

'Oh, my dear Lord.' Charlie slumped down onto the sofa bed. 'Three children within two years of marriage! That has to be a record.' Then he kissed Muriel's forehead. 'I guess I'm making up for lost time.'

'I know,' cried Muriel. 'And I'll still only be twenty. Plenty of years ahead for many more!'

'Oh, my dear Lord,' repeated Charlie.

He lost no time in explaining the situation at the factory, and was very glad he did. Not only was he going to get another raise, but there was a good chance that he would get a promotion to the position as assistant manager of the factory's tool and supply rooms, all four of them. If he got that position, it would mean yet another increase in salary, which would help him to not only support his growing family but also allow him to continue saving toward buying a home.

'That's wonderful news,' he told his manager. 'Muriel will be thrilled. And business must be booming.'

Heathfield nodded. 'It really is. I'm going to be needing a new payroll manager soon, especially if you keep getting pay rises at this rate. Sanders can't keep up with the general accounts and sort out all the wages.' He ran his hand through his hair distractedly. 'Sometimes we have to run just to keep up with ourselves.'

And Charlie had an idea.

'Mr Heathfield, would you consider employing another ex-prisoner?'

'Sure,' said the manager with a shrug, 'if he comes as well recommended as you.'

'He does,' Charlie assured him. 'There is one more thing, however. My friend is black.'

Heathfield stared at him for a long moment, then shrugged again. 'Charlie, if he knows enough about payroll and figures to get me out of this scrape, I don't care if he's green with yellow spots. Just get him in as soon as you can.'

'I will, sir. Thank you.'

Before he could lose another moment, Charlie called the prison and set about finding Amos. By the next day, Charlie had discovered that Amos was living back with his family in the town where he'd committed his crime all those years ago. On returning from the war, he'd found work in a storeroom, and was making a meager living on which to support his wife and their two growing children.

It was two hours' drive away, but Charlie wasn't prepared to wait. Borrowing Roger's car, he took to the open road with a thrill at driving at speed again, and made his way to Corville to track Amos down at his home.

When he opened the door, those familiar eyes gazed at Charlie just as they had decades before, and then the two men embraced like brothers.

'I didn't know you were out!' gasped Amos. 'How did you get out?'

'Did you not read my letters? You know me and my letters – I wrote you dozens of messages over the years.'

Amos frowned, puzzled. 'I got a few when I first landed in the Pacific, but they stopped after a year or so. The guys used to complain that the mail was hit and miss - unlike the Japanese.'

Charlie studied his friend closely. The war had taken its toll on Amos; he could see that. He looked fifteen years older than Charlie rather than six or seven, and life continued to be hard for him and his family, by the looks of it.

Well, all that was about to change.

'Amos, my friend,' he said, clapping the man on the arm, 'if you haven't read those letters, then we're going to be here a while. I have a lot – a *lot* – to tell you.'

'I ain't going nowhere,' said Amos with a grin.

'Oh, yes, you are.'

Where he'd stay, and how, they weren't quite sure. But Charlie knew, somehow, that they'd work it out.

It was all settled, and quickly. To celebrate his promotion and Amos' recruitment to the position of Payroll Manager, Charlie decided to take Muriel out for a night on the town. They headed downtown on Saturday, starting with a matinee movie, then a walk in the downtown rose-garden park, followed by a T-bone steak dinner at the best downtown restaurant. Before they went out on their date, Charlie took his very pregnant wife shopping.

It was evidently a very happy day for Muriel. As she pointed out on several occasions, she was married to a handsome, industrious and capable man; she had a beautiful, healthy daughter; she was on the verge of delivering twins; her husband had bought her a beautiful new coat and hat, which she wore to stares and compliments, on a wonderful date with a loving husband, and their future was very bright.

Charlie, too, very much enjoyed his date with his radiant wife, who looked especially beautiful in her new coat, hat and gloves. Life seemed incredibly sweet.

Finally, their twins were born: a healthy boy and girl. Everyone was surprised that it wasn't two boys or two girls. According to the doctor, Muriel had a very difficult time in delivering the twins. He recommended that she follow a program of prescribed medicine and rest as much as possible, and that she abstain from love-making for six months. Charlie, Betty, and Roger pitched in to help as much as they could with taking care of the twins, whom they named Charlotte (Char) and Charles III (Charlie).

As it turned out, Muriel recovered her strength faster than the doctor thought she would, and after a month she was feeling much stronger. The only problem she seemed to have was in nursing the twins. She'd had no trouble in nursing her first born, not moving her onto the bottle and solid foods until she was a little over six-months old. With the twins, however, she tried to nurse them one at a time, both at the same time, and alternating from one breast to the other. For a while it seemed that she was not even making enough milk for the both of them, and she supplemented her milk with bottled formula which meant that Charlie and the others could feed the babies too. Gradually, by the end of the second month, her milk production increased and they were able to settle into a routine.

During the two months in which Muriel was recovering and struggling with breast-feeding the twins, Charlie did little else but work at the factory and help out at home. After that, however, he started going fishing with Johnny again, to incredibly good effect. On one trip alone he brought home three large bass, the largest over two and a half pounds; two channel catfish, weighing a total of four pounds; a yellow catfish, weighing nearly eight pounds; and seven nice sized Bluegills. Whenever he cast his baited hook into the water, he had a fish on it in less than a minute.

Never before had he had so much fun fishing, especially when Amos was able to join him for the odd trip. Over the next four or so months, the fishing remained incredibly good, and the family had fish for supper four to five times a week. His fishing experiences during these months put the hook into him so solidly that his main hobby for the rest of his life would be fishing.

As the doctor ordered, Muriel and Charlie avoided making love for a full six months, but when they finally returned to it, it was clear to Charlie that Muriel was holding back, in pain, and clearly not enjoying herself. It was totally unlike their earlier experiences. It was discovered that her uterus was still not completely healed, and that she had an infection. She began a three-week-long antibiotic program, and had to avoid love-making for several more weeks. It was months before they resumed anything like their previous pattern, and Charlie often held back for fear he might hurt Muriel.

Eventually, though, Muriel and Charlie got back to the routine of working and taking care of their three children. Detty was two-years old, and getting into everything. The twins were nearly a year old, and showing signs that they would soon be walking around like their big sister. Charlie was working hard at his new job, having learned most of the ins and outs of the operation of being a salaried assistant manager rather than a piece-worker, and was enjoying it immensely. He liked his immediate supervisor, the tool and supply rooms manager.

It was the manager's primary job to keep the inventory of all tools and supplies; to dispose of all damaged tools; to be constantly on the lookout for better, more efficient tools, and to do the purchasing of supplies and tools. Part of Charlie's responsibilities on Mondays, in addition to managing and scheduling of the tool/supply rooms staff, was to assist the manager and learn his job, in case he was needed to take over the manager's job, because of sickness or anything else which might result in the manager's temporary absence. With regular sightings of Amos, despite his being squirreled away at the top of the stairs in the payroll office, Charlie's working life had become a true reflection of everything he'd learned in prison, and the innate qualities he had always developed within himself.

Things were humming along, as Charlie and Muriel settled into becoming old hands at married life and in raising a family. Charlie doted on his children, spending as many precious hours with them after work as he could. At week-ends he spent considerable amounts of time taking them on outdoor excursions, usually to a playground or park, with Muriel and sometimes her mother tagging along too as they pushed the children along in strollers or pulled them behind in wagons. Charlie loved being outdoors, feeling especially free and liberated after spending over half of his life in prison confinement. This special love for the outdoors undoubtedly contributed strongly to his love for fishing.

During these exceptionally harmonious times with his family and in his work at the factory, Charlie managed to get in one or two fishing excursions each month, and continued to have success in catching supplies.

Charlie had never been happier. He very much enjoyed his work at the factory; he loved and very much appreciated his little family; their savings account was growing, giving promise that they would soon be able to purchase their own home, and his marriage was still enjoyably passionate.

Then, a few months after their third wedding anniversary, Muriel announced that she thought that she was pregnant again. He was raised as a Catholic, and had come from a large family, so it was natural for him to want to have a large family himself.

Muriel, however, did not seem to share his happiness.

'Maybe this should be my last pregnancy,' she said suddenly one evening. 'We'll have four children before the end of our fourth year of marriage. That's twice the number of the family I come from.'

'But ... you said there was time for plenty more.'

Muriel scowled. 'Maybe I hadn't thought about what that would actually mean. More breast-feeding, more painful pregnancies, more difficult births.'

'I hadn't really given it much thought,' said Charlie, 'but when you put it like that, I can see what you mean.'

'And I keep losing my figure, Charlie. Do you know what that's like when I'm only in my early twenties? I don't want to keep losing my figure!'

Charlie slid his arms across her rounded belly. 'Your figure looks wonderful, when you're pregnant and when you're not.'

To his surprise, she pushed his hands away and flounced toward the door. 'Oh, you don't get it. How can you possibly get it?'

And Charlie had to admit that he probably couldn't.

He couldn't help thinking, though, that there was something more to it than just the fact of having more babies and a thickening waistline. Occasionally, Muriel seemed distracted, glancing out of the window as cars passed, and urging her mother to take her out to bingo more often. Charlie even wondered if she would prefer to go back to work rather than stay at home with the babies, although she'd never said as much.

There was definitely something a little off with her, though.

And Charlie knew it, because there was something a little off with him, too.

Somehow, implausibly and confusingly when he still adored his wife and their life together, Charlie had fallen head-over-heels in love with someone else.

And this time, the feeling of love was like nothing he had ever known before.

Chapter 8

Molly Moving On

*"They told me to take a streetcar named Desire
and then transfer to one called Cemeteries and ride six blocks
and get off at - Elysian Fields!"*

A Streetcar Named Desire, Tennessee Williams

Every morning, after breakfast and seeing her father and Tommy off to work, Molly's mind would work overtime about her situation. She hoped upon hope that Tommy's love-making would eventually become just that - *love* making.

She greatly feared, however, that it would not, and that the best she could do was to grin and bear it. If so, she was determined to do her wifely duty - to simply lie in bed and sexually "service" her husband. If this was to be the situation, she could only hope that their sexual episodes would decrease, considerably, in frequency.

Oh, how she wished she could talk to her mother about it. She didn't even want to bother Maureen with her woes. Her marriage with Tommy was nothing like her sister's relationship with Angus, so how could she possibly understand?

And so her dreary, unhappy life went on, made bearable by the presence of her father, caring for the animals they raised for eggs and meat, tending the family garden, and visiting with Carol (who never married and became a firm friend) several times a week.

Her father was re-elected as County Sheriff, and was spending more and more time in his job. Tommy was also working a lot of over-time. She was grateful that he seemed to fall upon a lot of the night shifts, which she enjoyed because of being able to sleep alone in her bed.

After she had been married about four years, her father's brother died suddenly of a heart attack, leaving her aunt, Dolores, destitute. Since there was plenty of room in their home, her father immediately invited her to move in with them. Not only did she readily accept the invitation, but since she was an excellent cook and housekeeper, it was natural that she took over most of Molly's duties. This left Molly with a lot of time on her hands, which she filled mainly by spending more time with Carol, and, at the urging of her father, by doing volunteer work in the community.

During this time, Tommy was spending less and less time at home, often staying out all night even when work did not demand it. Their sexual encounters continued to be rough affairs. She eventually came to characterize them in her mind as the copulation of goats: Molly was the nanny goat, and Tommy a billy goat who roughly mounted her, humped and bleated for a short while, and then just as roughly, dismounted her. Fortunately, their copulations became less and less frequent, until it became rare that they even slept together, let alone have intercourse. This was fine with her, though she began to have suspicions that Tommy might be seeing someone else.

John, the young sheriff in whom she'd been more interested, confirmed this for her when he brought Tommy home one morning in the patrol van, out of his mind on whiskey.

'How is he drunk?' she said, barely able to conceal her repulsion at the sorry state of her husband. 'I thought he'd been at work all night.'

'Not any work you'd care to know about,' muttered John in an undertone, but loud enough for Molly to hear him.

'What do you mean?'

John shook his head. 'I shouldn't be the one to tell you what your husband gets up to, Molly, but if it carries on I might have to arrest him, and then it'll be too late.'

'He's ... he's seeing someone, isn't he? My husband's having an affair. Don't worry, John, I was already aware of that.' Then she considered what John had just said. 'But ... you wouldn't arrest him for having an affair, because that's not sheriff's business, unless ...'

'Unless,' repeated John flatly, hardly able to meet her gaze. He turned his hat in his hands over and over, then finally let his words tumble out. 'I'm sorry, Molly, but Tommy has been exhibiting sexually deviant tendencies. We've all been aware of it, but most of us ignored it to spare you the humiliation. And your father, of course.'

It was the worst thing she could ever have imagined of her husband, but as she thought about his apparent disgust at the touch of her flesh, and the barbaric, brutal, Saturnalian assaults on her body, it all made sense. 'He's a ... a queer?'

John looked around him as if willing someone else to appear to answer her questions, then nodded. 'I'm sorry, Molly. Yes, he's queer. And he's going to have to be very careful or he'll lose his job.'

'And his wife,' said Molly bitterly.

'I think,' said John, scratching his nose, 'that maybe he lost his wife a long time ago.'

She watched John as he poured Tommy out onto the steps and drove away as fast as he could decently allow himself to go. Why had she permitted herself to be intimidated by this horrible man – and furthermore, why had John? Their lives could all have been very different.

She sighed and stepped over her husband's prone body. Let him sleep it off. Whatever 'it' was.

She began to seriously review their marriage, in an attempt to discover what had gone wrong. During their first year, she'd started to wonder why she was not getting pregnant, since they used no precautions. Also, she was puzzled by the fact that Tommy never mentioned children, and always seemed rather indifferent whenever the subject came up. The fact that Maureen ended up having three boys, all within the first six years of her marriage, added to her wonderment. Moreover, it seemed that all the young married couples in the area, except for them, were having babies. Naturally, her sister, her father, Carol, and many others inquired from time to time about whether she and Tommy planned to have children. She never knew how to answer them, so she always responded with a vague answer.

Now, in retrospect, she decided that the reason she never became pregnant was Tommy's fault. Perhaps the rumors were true, that he was queer and might, therefore, have faulty sperm. She had no idea, but this possibility made sense to her. She thought that his queerness might also explain his "billy-goat-like" method of sexual intercourse. Thus, rather than "normal" love-making with his wife, it might be that it was simply a form of queer masturbation.

Her plans to do anything about her hideous marriage were soon interrupted, however, when the Second World War broke out. This caused major changes in the area, most noticeably as the community emptied of men between the ages of eighteen and thirty.

Tommy did not enter the military because of his age, and because law-enforcement officers were generally exempted.

Molly could barely stand to look at him.

'You could have volunteered. You *should* have volunteered,' she told him when he said he wasn't enlisting.

'What I do is none of your business,' he growled.

But Molly had had enough. 'You'd like it, anyway,' she said venomously. 'All those men around. Is that why you became a sheriff, Tommy? Because of all that male camaraderie? If my father ever knew …'

For a moment, she thought he was about to strike her. Instead he turned on his heel and reappeared several minutes later with a suitcase.

'I don't know how I've put up with you for so long,' he spat as he passed her in the kitchen.

Molly didn't attempt to stop him. She heard later that he'd moved into a house with three other men, which convinced her that the queer rumors were substantiated - although Tommy never admitted that he was a sexual deviant.

He did, however, ask her for a divorce, which she gladly and quickly agreed to. To her mind, it was good riddance.

Since she was rid of Tommy, and since there was a severe shortage of workers in war-production plants, she decided that she would take a job in a nearby manufacturing plant, located only approximately 20 miles from her home.

There was no public transportation, so she purchased an automobile for commuting to work, and because she worked in a plant which produced essential war materials, she was given an extra ration of gasoline. Her father gave his blessing to her war-plant work, and also made it clear that he was glad that she had obtained a divorce from Tommy. Tommy continued to work as a deputy sheriff, although he kept his distance from Jesse after the divorce. However, the relationship between Tommy and her father eventually became strained when he ran against him for the job of County Sheriff. Her father won the election by a landslide, which made her exceedingly happy.

Her life settled into a routine for the remainder of the war years. She worked at least an eight-hour shift at the war plant, and while living at home she did mostly outside chores - feeding and watering the animals, tending the garden, picking fruit and vegetables, depending on the season. On weekends, she usually spent time with Carol and a few other friends.

She never dated, even though she was frequently asked out by men at the plant and a few from her neighborhood. She seemed to have no interest in men. Her lack of interest was undoubtedly related to her abominable marriage experiences, but besides that, nearly all the young men of her own age were either away serving their country in the military, or were married.

From time to time she thought about some of the men she dated or knew before she married Tommy. However, the two men – John and another deputy - that were not in the military were married, and the ones that were away serving their country were never home.

During the war, those serving in the military never got leave. They were in the service for the duration of the war. Even if they were wounded, they would be patched up and either sent back to combat duty or sent to support, or training duty, depending on the severity of their injuries. Molly had heard that a marine she knew was severely wounded while serving in the South Pacific. After treatment and rehabilitation in a navy hospital, he was sent to a stateside training facility, where he spent the rest of the war training recruits. However, military policy did not allow military personnel stationed Stateside to be treated any differently than those serving overseas. Even though this marine was stationed only a few hundred miles from his home, he was prohibited from taking leave or having visitors. It seemed an unnecessary level of hardship in a situation that was already unbearable.

After working at the plant for about a year, Molly was invited, along with another divorced woman co-worker, to move into a small house of another colleague whose husband was in the Army, serving in the European Theater of Operations. The two tenants would provide company for the lonely wife, and much-needed financial help to the newlyweds. Since she now lived close enough to walk to and from work, or to walk a few blocks and take a trolley car, Molly saved enough automobile and commuting expenses to nearly cover the costs of her rent and food. This continued to be Molly's living arrangements until a few months after the end of the war, and she welcomed the change from her circumstances with Tommy.

Other than living near the plant in town, the rest of her routine remained about the same. Nearly every weekend she stayed at her father's home, where she helped her father and aunt with chores around the garden, in the orchard and with the animals. Her weekend entertainment also generally remained the same as she continued to hang out with Carol and a few other girl-friends. As for men, she continued to shun them, concentrating instead on working as many hours at the plant as she could. Almost every week's pay check included considerable overtime, so she was able to continue saving a lot of money.

Finally, the war ended, and shortly after that her war-time role at the plant also closed. This was expected, since the plant guaranteed every service man their job back when they were discharged. Of course, there were quite a few who did not return, but this was no help to the women employees in keeping their jobs, because the plant also had an aggressive policy of giving first choice of their open jobs to other returning veterans.

Molly's landlord's husband returned home, safe and sound, so Molly moved back to her father's home. All in all, she was happy. The war was over, most of the men had returned, and she was able to relax for the first time in a long time, now that she was free from her intense work routine. It suited her, for now, to be unemployed and to be able to work with the plants and animals on her father's "mini-farm."

Her relaxed, easy life did not last long, however. She'd been home only three weeks when she received a call from one of the women she had worked with at the war plant.

'Hey, doll, it's Vonnie,' said her former colleague. 'What are you up to?'

'Nothing much, to be honest,' replied Molly.

'That's great! 'Cos I wanted to ask if you'd be interested in coming back to work at the plant.'

Molly stared at her reflection in the mirror over the hall table. It looked calm and capable, but not very interesting at all.

What had happened to the young woman who tossed baseballs with the guys, and flirted with Freddie Carter at the traveling fair? It all seemed a long time in the past.

But that girl? Yes, she'd have been interested in going back to work.

'I thought all the jobs were gone now the boys are back.'

'Yeah,' sneered Vonnie, 'apart from the ones they don't want to do. My boss is hiring women for certain roles – the ones that don't pay so much.'

It turned out that the plant had received some large, long-term contracts with the War Department, manufacturing critical military items that were needed to build up depleted inventories.

Vonnie had mentioned Molly to her new boss and, on the basis of her recommendation, he decided to hire her without going through the normal interview process.

If she was interested.

The girl – no, the woman – in the mirror gazed back at her. What was there to think about? After discussing it with her father, she called the manager and took the job.

Chapter 9

A Special Courtship

Never thought my heart could be so yearny.
Why did I decide to roam?
Gonna take that sentimental journey –
Sentimental journey home

Sentimental Journey, Bing Crosby

On her first day of work, Molly was told to go to the office of her boss for orientation.

'I'm George,' said The Boss.

'We spoke the other evening.'

'That's right. Vonnie recommended you.'

Molly smiled. 'She's very kind.'

'That's right. We like kind people here. I think I'm quite kind myself,' said George, smiling back at her.

After inquiring about how she made it to work that snowy morning, he spent a few minutes going over her duties. He then started to ask questions about herself and her situation, reiterating that anytime she needed a ride to or from work, he would be more than happy to take her. He told her that he was single and had plenty of spare time. Molly didn't volunteer any information about her own situation.

'What's your experience with motorcycles?' he asked suddenly.

'None whatsoever. Is that part of the job?'

'No! I just like them.'

She was teasing him just a little, but then, he was asking an awful lot of questions: why she lived so far away from the factory; what her previous job had been at the plant; what work she'd done during the war.

'I'm new to this plant myself,' he told her, 'having previously worked for another metal manufacturing plant which also made critical military products during the war.'

'Then I'm sure you'll be great to work for,' said Molly.

A bell clanged in the distance, and George suddenly sprang to attention. 'Is that the time? I'm sorry, Molly, I didn't mean to keep you so long. You'd better be off now, but how about we have lunch together in the plant's cafeteria to continue our conversation?'

She accepted his invitation, and reminded him – kindly – that she already knew where the cafeteria was.

On her way back to her office, she wondered about her meeting with her new boss. He was certainly friendly - very friendly, in fact. Kind, like he'd said. His personal questions and comments were simply intended to make her feel comfortable in her new job, and to impress upon her that he was very accessible to the employees under his supervision. He had said that he was single. She wondered whether he had ever been married. He appeared to be in his late thirties or early forties. He did not mention children, although she volunteered that she had no children from her nearly six-year-long marriage.

She spent the next few hours being oriented to the facilities in her office, her work responsibilities, and the locations of other offices and facilities which she would visit from time to time as a matter of course in her work. Before she knew it, it was time for lunch, and she was escorted to the cafeteria by her two office co-workers.

George was already there, and motioned for her to join him at his table once she'd chosen her food. He got up and assisted her into a chair at the table.

As they ate, their conversation picked up where it left off at their morning meeting in George's office. They shared more information about themselves.

George had never been married, apparently - he simply never found the right woman. During the war, he was exempted from the draft because of his age, and several attempts to enlist in the Army Air Forces failed because of how old he was and his employment in a critical war industry.

He brought up the subject of motorcycles again. He had been a motorcycle buff since shortly after graduating from high school. He presently owned a big Harley, which was less than a year old, and a classic Indian, which he owned since he was in his early twenties. He frequently rode his Harley, often riding it to work when the weather was good. He also rode it to motorcycle races on the weekends. He didn't ride his Indian often, and when he did, it was mostly to special events such as classic gatherings and shows. The Indian was his pride and joy, and he kept it in pristine condition.

'I'm talking a lot,' he said with a laugh. 'Do you always make people do that?'

'Not usually.' Molly smiled. 'They're normally trying to get a word in edgewise.'

George had the grace to blush. 'I'm so sorry. Let me make it up to you. Perhaps you would consider going riding with me sometime when the weather improves.'

She said she would think about it, and headed out of the cafeteria before anyone could cry 'favoritism'. Jesse had taught her well.

Over the next several months Molly settled into her job. Although her main responsibilities involved ordering and inventory, her overall work was especially enjoyable because she did a variety of things and worked with numerous people during a typical week. She saw George nearly every day, and joined him for lunch once or twice a week, mostly to discuss "work-related issues."

She was becoming fond of George. He was a nice guy and a very good boss. All her co-workers loved working for him, and a few of the girls obviously had a romantic interest in him, agreeing that George would be a good catch.

Molly, however, was not particularly interested in being the one to catch him. According to her co-workers, George was 46 years old and had never been married. They said that even though he seemed to be a confirmed bachelor he regularly dated women, although never any of those who worked for him. In fact, they said, he rarely even dated women who worked anywhere else in the plant. That was a man who didn't want to be pinned down, in her opinion – and she'd had enough experience of that already.

At lunch one day, George asked her if she would like to go riding on a motorcycle with him some Saturday or

Sunday. It was late Spring, the days were getting warmer and warmer, and he was beginning to ride more often.

'I've never ridden on a motorcycle,' she said. 'I'm a little apprehensive.'

'You'll be safe with me. I've been riding for more than twenty-five years and never had an accident.'

'Well ... then I'm sure it will be fine.'

George grinned. 'Would you like to come to the motorcycle races? Might as well jump right in.'

'I've never attended races of any kind – oh, apart from some sulky horse races at the county fair, but I never paid much attention to them.'

'I don't think you'll find them much alike. Motor vehicle races are nothing like horse races. Car races are much more exciting - and motorcycle racing even more so.' He watched her reactions carefully. 'I will admit, though, that motor vehicle races are very much noisier than horse races.'

'In that case,' said Molly with a laugh, 'I'd better bring a large hat to tie down over my ears.'

On Saturday morning, she was having coffee with her father and aunt when they heard a motorcycle coming up their long driveway.

Her father went to the window. 'That is one big, shiny, black Harley,' he said, rather enviously. 'But why's he carrying a shopping bag?'

'Maybe he brought breakfast.'

Molly opened the door and quickly introduced George to her father and Aunt Dolores. He accepted their invitation to join them for some home-made apple pie and coffee.

'Ah. So it's not breakfast in the bag.'

George winked. 'Open it and see.'

Intrigued, Molly opened the bag. On top was a pair of leather trousers and a pair of fur-lined leather gloves, followed by a fleece-lined leather jacket. Underneath it all was a heavy leather helmet and a pair of goggles. It was brand new stuff, accompanied by a nice leather smell.

'You'll need to wear these to be safe and comfortable on the motorcycle.' George drained his coffee. 'That is excellent pie, ma'am.'

Aunt Dolores simpered like a young girl. Both she and Jesse were very impressed that George was so thoughtful, and they liked him immediately.

Molly excused herself to go to her room to put on her motorcycle gear. Aunt Dolores went with her, and helped her dress. She was somewhat self-conscious in her new outfit, which fit her almost to a T, which was surprising to her because she was exceptionally tall and had given no size measurements to George.

'Your outfit matches George's!' giggled Aunt Dolores.

'Not quite,' said George, appearing in the hallway. 'Mine's not nearly as fetching.'

Before leaving, George helped her adjust her helmet and showed her how to wear her goggles. He showed her how to best hang on and where to place her feet for maximum safety and comfort. Before she knew it, they were out on the road and roaring away from her house.

It didn't take long to become less anxious and even reasonably comfortable riding behind George. Of course, there was no chance of conversation between them because of the roar of the engine and the rush of the wind. As she relaxed she began to pay attention to the scenic vistas rushing by as they roared down the road. It was amazing to her how much more beautiful and clear the landscapes looked from the open-air viewpoint of the motorcycle as compared to riding in an automobile. She also began to become aware of how smooth the motorcycle rode and how well and solid it performed along the surface of the road.

The road passed by one small farm after another. It was a very pleasant and enjoyable scene of pretty farm houses, surrounded by neat, well-maintained barns and other outbuildings, all set within bucolic fields of grazing animals and colorful brown to black tilled fields; some containing crops in various stages of growth. Every ten to fifteen minutes, George would slow down as they proceeded through pretty little villages and towns. She was conscious of nearly everyone, walking along the sidewalks in the downtown areas of these neat little communities, gawking at them as they went by.

It was a beautiful, warm, sunny day, and although the wind blowing by them was chilly, it was invigorating. Dressed in her leather motorcycle outfit, she was comfortably warm. As they were pulling out of the fifth or sixth little town on their route, she was suddenly overwhelmed by a thrill, a feeling of joy. She hadn't felt this good in years, if ever.

Molly was basking in the glow of her euphoria, when suddenly she became aware of a din of engine and crowd noises, which they were rapidly approaching on their right front. She soon saw the source of the noise as George slowed down to turn into the grounds surrounding the racetrack. The grounds were a sea of people, most of them dressed as she and George were, surging around more motorcycles than she had ever seen in her lifetime, interspersed among the many pickup trucks and automobiles.

As George pulled into an area of parked motorcycles, he was greeted by the many men and women standing around their "bikes." It was obvious to Molly that he was well-known. He parked his bike and, as soon as the two of them dismounted, they were surrounded by a large crowd of people, all of them curious about who George had brought with him to the races. George introduced her to the crowd, and they responded with a warm, enthusiastic welcome.

After chatting for a few minutes, the crowd began to move, en masse, toward the spectator bleachers. As soon as they reached the edge of the stands, the crowd began to separate as individuals and small groups began to go to their seats. George escorted her to two seats located midway up and in the center of the stands. They had excellent seats from which to observe the races.

As soon as they were seated, George handed her a program and began to give her details - amidst the roar of motorcycles and the chattering din of the crowd - about the different races and about many of the individuals in each of them. He seemed to know many of the racers personally, and was quite knowledgeable about their abilities and prospects. If betting were allowed, George would easily win a lot of money.

During the races, Molly didn't join in the cheering and booing emanating from the crowd and from George, but rather sat back and casually took it all in. She enjoyed herself, even though she was not particularly excited by the races themselves. The overall atmosphere, and the obvious enthusiasm and enjoyment shown by George, was enough for her.

After the races, they slowly walked back to where George had parked his motorcycle, gradually being joined by others whose bikes were parked in the same area, who seemed to talk as one about the details and outcomes of the races.

'I see she's new, George,' cried a man in flamboyant navy leathers. 'Congratulations! She's a fine one.'

George looked puzzled. 'Not that new. I've had her months, Edgar. You've seen her before.'

Edgar grinned toward Molly. 'I wasn't talking about the bike.'

'Ah, you mean my new girlfriend. Yes, this is Molly.'

He showed her off with evident pride, and Molly grinned delightedly as George started up his bike. It was official! She situated herself behind him and adjusted her helmet and goggles, and they slowly made their way toward the gate, waving goodbye to everyone before they roared out onto the road toward her home.

The trip home was even more pleasurable then the trip to the track earlier. The day was still sunny and balmy, with a crystal-clear blue sky, and Molly was very content as they roared along the road. The pastoral landscape of agricultural fields, grazing animals, and neat farmsteads seemed even more beautiful than before. George's beautiful motorcycle, and their matching shiny black outfits, made her feel special. She was feeling quite content indeed, by the time they reached her home.

Both Jesse and Aunt Dolores, alerted by the roar of the motorcycle as they turned into their driveway, were outside to greet them as they parked and dismounted. During supper, Jesse and, especially Aunt Dolores, peppered George with questions which he answered amiably. Jesse was particularly interested in George's motorcycle and his many years of experience with motorcycles and racing. The food was delicious, and George appeared to gorge himself, asking for seconds, or even thirds, of nearly everything. They were absolutely sated when they retired to the living room to sit a spell. Molly could not remember ever eating so much. Moreover, she could not remember a time when she had such a thoroughly enjoyable day.

After a few minutes of conversation, George stood up. 'I really should be going,' he announced. 'I'd like to get home before dark.'

'Of course,' they said together.

Molly took him by the arm. 'Thank you for a truly wonderful day. I've never experienced anything quite like it.'

'Me neither,' said George. He smiled as she felt her cheeks redden. 'I look forward to discussing it all over again at lunch on Monday.'

'Lunch on Monday,' she agreed.

They all walked him down to his motorcycle and watched him as he rode out onto the road, waving as he roared away. As soon as they went back into the house, Jesse and Aunt Dolores began to grill her about her outing with George. She gave them all the details, and, as she did, she became increasingly aware that George was a very good person, and that she was beginning to like him very much.

On Monday, George met her as she went into the cafeteria at noon, and escorted her to the food line. As they approached the cashier, he told her that he was buying. She was his guest, he told her, and, therefore, lunch was on him. They recounted their favorite tales of the motorcycle before George took in a deep breath.

'Molly, would you consent to having dinner with me at the Palace Dinner Theater next Saturday night? The Bob Crosby orchestra will be playing and Bing Crosby and the Andrews Sisters are singing.'

She couldn't believe her ears. Those four singers were the nation's most famous icons of the recent war era. 'I would love to!'

She wanted to tell everyone in her office that George was taking her to the Palace on Saturday, but she was still afraid to say anything about it to anyone at the plant. She was certain that employees dating their bosses, if not against company policy, was certainly frowned upon. She kept it to herself, but could hardly wait to get home to tell her father and aunt about it.

She bounded through the door when she got home, to be greeted by Aunt Dolores who was overwhelmed by the prospect of such starry company. When he came home, Jesse heard the news and explained that many stars of stage and screen were still touring the country promoting the sale of war bonds. Even though the war in Europe had been over for over a year, and the war in the Pacific for more than nine months, the Nation had racked up a considerable debt, and there were plans to continue raising money through the sale of bonds until the debt was mostly paid off. As they had during the war itself, stars were volunteering their time and talent to help their country out. They considered it their patriotic duty.

'That's an incredible date, however, Molly,' said Jesse. 'It speaks well of George's intentions. I think it's entirely likely George may end up asking you to marry him.'

'It's our second date, Dad,' said Molly. 'Let's not get too excited.'

But ever since George asked her out, Molly had been thinking the same thing. Although most people she knew considered that George was definitely a confirmed bachelor, his behavior toward her since they first met on her first day of work did not match such a conclusion. After their outing at the races last week end she began to feel that George could be in love with her, and she began to entertain thoughts that she might be falling in love with him. His asking her out for a very special date at the Palace only reinforced these feelings

Molly began preparations for her night out with George as soon as breakfast was finished on Saturday morning. He'd said he would pick her up at 4:30, so she had a good eight hours to get ready. First off, Aunt Dolores began to do her hair, then she put on her make-up, admiring her image in the mirror. She felt that her aunt did the best job ever with her hair; that her new lipstick (which matched the color of her new dress) was the prettiest that she had ever worn; and that, overall, she had never looked better.

'Listen to yourself, Molly! So vain,' she whispered, but she knew that it was time. Time to feel okay about everything that had happened.

With an hour to go until George would arrive, she put on her new dress, which she had purchased for the occasion three days earlier. It complimented her tall, lithe and shapely figure very well. Feeling satisfied with herself and yet a little anxious, she went down stairs to wait for George in the living room with her father and aunt.

They were engrossed in an excited conversation when they were startled by a knock on the front door. They were surprised that they had not heard a vehicle drive up their driveway. But here was George at the door.

Jesse opened the door, and George stepped in, resplendently dressed in a black suit, set off by a crisp white shirt, a fancy, black bow tie, and expensive-looking, shiny black shoes. With his neatly cut and combed, graying black hair, he presented an imposing picture of a very handsome gentleman. Molly's heart did a flip; she was Cinderella being picked up by the handsome Prince Cary Grant, ready to whisk her off to the event of a lifetime.

Arriving at the Palace, George drove around in front of the entrance, where valets were waiting to park the car. This was Molly's first experience of valet parking. George opened the door for her and escorted her to the entrance, where a doorman greeted them and opened the door. As they stepped inside, the maitre d' escorted them to their table and seated them.

The table was beautifully decorated with a vase of red and white carnations and an ornate silver bucket of iced champagne. At Molly's place, there was a beautiful corsage of orchids. As soon as they were seated the Maitre d' pinned the corsage to Molly's dress, and cut one of the white carnations from the vase and placed it in the lapel of George's suit. He then poured each of them a glass of the chilled champagne, describing its brand and vintage as the bubbles fizzed into the glass. Next, he presented each of them with a large tasselled menu, announcing that he would soon return to take their orders.

George sat across from Molly with a look of admiration plastered across his face. Molly was all smiles as he picked up his champagne glass to offer a toast.

'To a beautiful evening, and a beautiful girl,' he said almost reverently.

Molly laughed. 'To a beautiful evening,' she agreed.

'We're very lucky.' George sipped from his champagne glass. 'This is one of the last benefit shows the Crosbys will be doing for the sale of war bonds. They and the Andrews Sisters have given many performances during the war years, raising considerable amounts of money to finance the costs of the war effort, but they'll stop them altogether soon.'

'So lucky,' said Molly, thinking 'in more ways than one' but keeping that to herself.

They both opted for the Palace's famous T-Bone steak - him the large cut and her the smaller one - preceded by an appetizer of oysters on the half-shell, followed by an acorn squash soup and a house salad, and it seemed to Molly that it was no time at all when their food began to arrive. The oysters, which she sprinkled liberally with pepper, were simply delicious, as were the soup and salad. The aroma emanating from the T-Bone steak, was out of this world, and it was the best tasting steak she had ever eaten. The delicious potatoes and asparagus were highly complementary to the steak. Almost as soon as she took her last bite, the maitre d' was there to take their dessert order. She ordered the suggested custard pudding, which was delicious, while George had the apple cobbler ala mode. This was followed, finally, by a glass of brandy, which punctuated the most divine and, without question, the most romantic meal she had ever had.

It was time to go to the theater, which had an entrance off the dining room. George came around to assist Molly from her chair, and escorted her to their seats, which were impressively located in the middle of the auditorium and about ten rows from the stage - a perfect location to enjoy the show. The ornate beauty of the theater combined with the perfect location of their seats, made her feel very special indeed.

And the show was wonderful, far exceeding her expectations. There were very few, if any, songs performed which she had not heard before on the radio or from record recordings. Both Bing Crosby and the Andrews Sisters had been exceptionally popular since the late thirties, especially during the war. The Bob Crosby orchestra was also popular, and was recently becoming even more so with the growing national popularity of swing band music. She simply loved the music that she was experiencing at the show, and could never have dreamed that she would be seeing these famous performers in person. The songs were divided between "Der Bing" and the Andrews Sisters, and they also sang some of their most popular duets, among them "You Made Me Love You," "I'll Be Seeing You", "Boogie Woogie Bugle Boy," and "Don't Sit Under the Apple Tree".

As soon as the show was over, Molly expected that they would leave, but George suggested that they finish the evening with a drink in the Cocktail Lounge. There they went to a table, decorated with a vase of carnations and an ornate silver iced-champagne bucket.

George helped to seat her and then took the opposite chair.

'Molly,' he said seriously, 'this has been the most enjoyable and memorable night of my life, and I hoped that you enjoyed it as much as I.'

'It's beyond words,' replied Molly.

George beckoned a nearby waiter to the table to pour their champagne

'Another toast.' George raised his glass. 'To the most incredible evening of our lives.' Then, reaching into his jacket pocket, George pulled out a small box containing the most dazzling diamond ring she had ever seen. 'So far,' he added softly.

At her side, he knelt on one knee, placed the ring on the ring-finger of her left hand, and asked, sincerely: "Will you marry me, and be my loving wife forever and ever?"

It was a spectacular ending to a Cinderella-like evening and without hesitating Molly said: "Yes, I will!"

He then gently pulled her to him and kissed her. They drove home with her very close beside him, instead of over in the middle of the passenger seat, as she had on the drive to the Palace. All the way to her home, he chatted with her about the events of the evening, and how pleased he was that good fortune had brought them together, and that she'd agreed to marry him. She made it clear that she felt exactly the same way, hugging the delight she felt to herself.

When they arrived at her home, the lights were on in the living room and kitchen. Her father and aunt were still up, waiting for her to come home. George escorted her up the steps to the door, and just as she was about to insert her key in the door, it opened to reveal her smiling father and aunt.

Molly held up her hand so that they could admire her spectacular engagement ring, and Aunt Dolores screamed.

'When?' they both asked. 'When will the wedding take place?"

They responded together, almost simultaneously.

"Soon!"

It was approaching midnight when George got up to leave. She went with him to the door, and after embracing him with a passionate kiss, she watched as he got into his car, drove out the driveway, and turned onto the road.

'It's magic,' she told the starlit sky. 'Sheer magic. And I hope it never ends.'

Chapter 10

The Star-Spangled Wedding

"What is it you want, Mary? What do you want? You want the moon? Just say the word and I'll throw a lasso around it and pull it down. Hey. That's a pretty good idea. I'll give you the moon, Mary."

George Bailey in It's a Wonderful Life

Molly arrived at work early on Monday, concerned about how they would tell their colleagues about their impending marriage. She went directly to George's office, and was surprised at how open he was with her as they held each other and kissed.

'Aren't you worried about how the manager will react?' she said, once she'd caught her breath.

George grinned, looking about as far from worried as could be. 'Not really,' he said, 'because I don't work here any more.'

'You ... you don't?'

'About a year ago, the manager at the factory on the other side of town tracked me down and offered me a job. I refused at the time, but when you accepted my proposal, I gave him a call and asked if the position was still available.' George inspected Molly's engagement ring, obviously quite pleased with himself. 'So we won't be in the same department in the same factory, and I won't be your boss as well as your husband. And the new job pays better and is closer to home.'

'It's a wonder you didn't take the job last year – it sounds perfect!'

'I didn't have you last year,' said George earnestly. 'Now, it's perfect.'

'And I can show off my ring!'

'You certainly can.'

That was no bad thing, considering that the wedding had been set for 4th July which was less than two months away. They'd agreed this date for several reasons: it was a holiday, so their family members and friends could more conveniently attend; it would be an opportunity for the two of them to express their patriotism in a very special way, and significantly, it heralded one of the biggest motorcycle races of the year - and, perhaps, they would be able to work their wedding and wedding reception in with this great event. 'And you'll never forget our anniversary,' Molly had joked.

Now, as soon as Molly got to her nearby office, she held up her left hand to show off her beautiful engagement ring. Everyone oohed and aahed over it, and although many were surprised to hear that her fiancé was George, they all expressed their congratulations and pleasure. If the "confirmed bachelor" was getting married, they were glad that it was to one of their own.

They went about informing everyone of their engagement throughout the day, and then began the serious discussion of where the wedding would take place. At lunch, the next day, George reported some good news. That morning, he'd had a meeting with Benjamin, his friend and manager of the racetrack, about the possibility of both the wedding and reception being held there. Ben had agreed enthusiastically, as it would fit in wonderfully with the spectacular program which was being planned for the first 4th of July since the end of the war.

George was even more excited by the prospect of the wedding than Molly – perhaps, she thought, because it was his first.

'I know the owner of a company which specializes in custom-made motorcycle outfits,' he said, sketching designs on a work-pad. 'What do you think to us wearing matching bike gear? I'm sure he could make it classy enough for a wedding and patriotic enough for a 4th of July celebration.' He glanced up from his sketching. 'Or … did you want a white dress and all that?'

'I've had all that,' said Molly, quite content to let George lead. 'I want whatever you want.'

So George and Ben planned and organized. The wedding ceremony would occur during the half-time ceremonies between the morning and afternoon races, and the reception would be held in the track's clubhouse during the two-hour break. It was to be a very patriotic theme race day, honoring the area's veterans by encouraging them to wear their uniforms and decorations, and providing free admission and lunches for themselves and all members of their families. Admission for the evening program and fireworks would be free and completely open to the public, and all of this was to be made possible by donations from local companies.

George agreed to pay a substantial proportion of the total costs, in compensation for accommodating the wedding ceremony and reception, again with free admission and lunches. He asked Jesse to be his best man, and Carol, with whom Molly had remained close friends, was to be maid of honor.

George was certain that both of their factories and some of the factory's suppliers would make contributions to help pay for the veterans and their families' admission to the event and the cost of their lunches. Within a couple of weeks, George had raised more than half the funds needed to pay for the entire event from Molly's factory, his factory, and many of the factory's suppliers, with the suggestion that if there was more money raised than was needed to cover the costs, they give the excess to either the USO or use it to buy war bonds to help pay for the country's remaining war debt. His philanthropy and commitment to the veterans was above and beyond anything that Molly had ever experienced before, and she was warmed through by a quiet pride in her husband-to-be.

On the Sunday before the 4th of July, after one of Aunt Dolores' famous dinners, Molly and George tried on their well-tailored, white linen outfits, beautifully trimmed with red and blue designs. Both suits had a spectacular large, spread-winged, bald eagle embroidered on the back. They fit beautifully, with Molly's set off by a veiled bridal tiara and George's with a handsome red, white and blue boater, and finished off with white boots. George would drive the two of them, the outfits, and Jesse and Dolores to the track in his Cadillac, and there they would be met by two hundred family members and friends at the wedding and reception spread across the prime sections around the clubhouse. Everything was now set for the wedding.

The 4th of July dawned bright and balmy, with the promise of a warm day filled with sunshine. Just before breakfast, Carol knocked on the door.

'How's the blushing bride?' asked Carol with a nudge.

'Not blushing, just excited.'

Molly had never told Carol about her life with Tommy, as she was his sister when all was said and done, but Carol knew enough to be excited for her.

Carol gave Molly a hug. 'He's a good man,' she said, without adding "unlike Tommy" but pausing long enough to make her meaning clear to her friend. 'You'll be very happy.'

And Molly believed it to the center of her heart. How could she not be completely ecstatic every day of her life from now on, with this wonderful man lavishing such loving attention on her? No woman could ask for more, apart from children, of course – and hopefully they would come soon, too.

After a hearty breakfast and a pre-wedding embrace with her bridegroom, the five of them set off in George's car, in time to get there a half-hour before the 9:00 opening. On arriving at the VIP parking area, they were met by a track official and escorted to the clubhouse. As they were putting their wedding things away, Ben came in to give a quick update.

'Every seat occupied,' he declared gleefully, 'and fifteen percent profit for war bonds. Can you believe it?' He slapped George on the shoulder. 'It's three quarters veterans and their families, and they'll be participating in the parades and ceremonies. It's going to be quite a day!'

'And there's a wedding to enjoy,' Jesse reminded him.

Ben laughed. 'As if I'd forget! It's truly a wonderful 4th of July.'

He gave them copies of the program as he excused himself from the room and they went to find their seats for the start of opening ceremonies. Their seats were in the center, about half-way between the clubhouse and the portable stage that was wheeled out in front of them and on which the wedding ceremony would take place.

The track announcer declared the day's festivities open. Almost immediately, far down the track to the left, the famous band from the area's university struck up a Sousa march, and began marching toward the grandstand. Behind the band was a very large number of veterans, in the uniforms of the various branches of the armed services, marching twelve abreast.

'All the veterans here are holders of the Purple Heart, ladies and gentleman,' announced the MC. 'Let's salute their courage and patriotism.'

'Goodness, George,' whispered Molly, fighting back tears. 'This is the most extraordinary day.'

'A day to count our blessings.' George dropped a kiss on Molly's hair, watching the ceremony intently. A good man, she repeated to herself. A very good man.

On command, the parade halted. They all turned a right face as the band played the national anthem, while the flag was raised to the top of the flagpole. This was followed by three benedictions delivered by a minister, a priest and a rabbi. At the end of the benedictions, the band struck up a medley of the songs of the four major branches of the armed services as the parade marched to the right down the track.

The grandstand was then wheeled away, and the morning program of four races began. All four races were very competitive and exciting, with only three accidents, one in the second and two in the third and no serious injuries. The second race was the most exciting of all, with every one of the eight riders having the lead at least once. Immediately after the fourth race, the grandstand was wheeled back out in front-center of the clubhouse seats.

While this was taking place George, Molly, Jesse and Carol made their way up into the clubhouse to change into their wedding outfits, as the M.C. introduced the second parade of veterans from every one of the services who were the Honored Heroes of the day. They were all decorated with medals awarded for valor in combat, ranging from the Bronze Star to the Army Distinguished Service Cross and Navy Cross; over half were also decorated with the Purple Heart.

As the Marine Band played, the Commanding General of the state's National Guard walked to the microphone. He himself was a hero of both the First and Second World Wars: awarded the Bronze Star and Purple Heart in WWI and Distinguished Service Medal, Legion of Merit, Bronze Star and Purple Heart in WWII. As soon as the band stopped playing, the General then delivered a stirring speech, the first of several which would meet with thunderous applause.

Then, on cue, an organist began playing the "Wedding March" on the clubhouse organ. As it blared out of the speakers throughout the racetrack, the five members of the wedding party made their way down to the grandstand.

The wedding ceremony lasted about ten minutes, and the crowd was rapt and very quiet while it was taking place. The wedding party was colorfully radiant, with the Minister (the same uncle who had married Molly and Tommy) wearing a white robe, a white and gold sash, and a woven gold belt, the bride and groom in their custom made white motorcycle suits, with the eagle on the back and trimmed in red and blue, Jesse in a very nice, pin-striped, dark-grey suit, and Carol in a well-fitting pink dress set off with a veiled, coral-colored hat. When the crowd heard Molly say, "I do," they broke out in a raucous applause, which was repeated when the Minister introduced the newly-weds to the audience.

The Minister returned to the clubhouse to shed his robes, while the other four members of the wedding party made their way to their seats to re-join Aunt Dolores and enjoyed their box lunch. They remained in their wedding raiment as they watched the remaining races and closing ceremonies, so that they would be dressed for the reception.

The four afternoon races were about as exciting as the morning ones. In all of them the leads changed hands frequently, and the finishes were very close. In fact, in two of them the top three finishers were bunched: with less than a motorcycle length between first and third place. A few minutes after the 8th race, the grandstand was again wheeled out and put in place. The M.C. then stepped to the mike and requested that all veterans at the track should leave their seats, and assemble behind the Marine Corps band down the track to the left of the grandstand. Next, he introduced the last two speakers of the day: a Lieutenant Colonel Navy Nurse Corps veteran and, the celebrity attraction of the day - the movie star, Colonel Jimmy Stewart, a decorated bomber pilot in the European Theater of WWII.

The Lieutenant Colonel spoke simply and to great effect.

'With so many veterans here, I'm sure they would all join me in recognizing the vital contributions made by women in the services and back here at home during the war. Nurses, mechanics, cooks, auxiliary staff – the war could not have been won without them. Without the women working in defense plants, building the planes, tanks, trucks, jeeps, and other vital war materials, the war could have been lost. They are the unsung heroines of the war, and I commend them all.'

Molly wiped away another tear. This really had to be the most unusual wedding day, but somehow it seemed to sum up what everyone had gone through, and why they had fought so hard for this freedom.

Colonel James Stewart then stepped to the mike, to deafening shouts and clapping.

'I can't really add much to what the Lieutenant Colonel has already said.' His voice, so familiar to everyone, was close to breaking as he viewed the masses of veterans before him. 'It's simply an honor to be here, and to have fought at your side. God bless us all.'

Then he stood dramatically to attention and turned his head to the left, as the Marine Corps band broke out into a rousing rendition of, "The Washington Post," and began marching toward the grandstand area. Behind the band marched every veteran at the track, led by the female veterans of all services. The band led the formation of veterans down the center of the track, halting when the center of the veteran's formation was directly in front of the bandstand. The band then wheeled around to take a position directly behind the middle of the veteran's formation, while the color guard rearranged itself so that the American Flag was at the front, followed by the service flags. The band then played stirring renditions of Cohan's, "You're A Grand Old Flag," and Sousa's "Stars and Stripes Forever."

Colonel Stewart saluted. 'Our country, in fact the whole world, must remember every day the service and sacrifices made by these veterans assembled here. We must remember every day the sacrifices made by the families of these veterans – please, all of you, stand up so we can see you. Yes! We honor you all.' He led the applause for the startled families of the veterans. 'And finally, I would like to thank those responsible for giving me the privilege and honor of being a part of this very impressive patriotic program. I'm currently on a USO tour to raise money for blind veterans, and I must say, I have never been so proud to stand up for our country. Thank you.'

Jimmy Stewart walked away to a standing ovation, before the track was cleared for the feature race, pitting the winners of the eight earlier races against each other.

The feature race was the most exciting one of all. It had a lot of drama as the eight racing daredevils maneuvered, and careened down the track. The lead changed 27 times, with only a few minor mishaps, and all eight riders finished the race. On next to the last lap, the favorite to win the race, broke away from his nearest competitors blasted forward, winning in track-record time. After taking a victory lap, the winner then made his way to the grandstand where Colonel Stewart presented him with a beautiful, large trophy.

Finally, everything in the clubhouse was set up for the reception. A serving line was in place for a buffet-style dinner, featuring southern-fried chicken, baked ham, corn-on-the-cob, mashed potatoes, green beans, sliced tomatoes and cucumbers in vinegar, bread pudding, and two cobblers - apple and cherry. Refreshments included iced tea, iced water, coffee, milk, lemon-aid, and draft beer. Long tables with benches, each seating twelve people, were arranged in four rows of four tables each, with another one set up as a head table. It seemed that nearly all, if not all, of the people who were invited to the reception had showed up. With everyone hugging each other and laughing at the novelty of the day, the clubhouse was quite crowded.

The reception went well, with George and Molly doing their best to greet, chat with, and accept congratulations from everyone there. They were pleased to see that nearly all their relatives and friends who had served in the military were wearing their uniforms. After approximately a half-hour of circulating around the room, Jesse and Aunt Dolores, along with Uncle Albert, formally introduced George and Molly, and made a few brief remarks about the wedding, as well as about the wonderful events which they were witnessing at the racetrack.

The two hours went by so fast that they were surprised when someone said that there was only fifteen minutes left until the start of the evening program. The clubhouse began to empty, as all those staying returned to their seats to watch the Army drill team, the parade of nine local school bands and the extravagant firework display.

The wedding party, however, decided to leave before the display began. On the way home, even though they were tired, all five chatted away about the remarkable things which had taken place at the racetrack, and how privileged they felt that the wedding had been a part of it. It was, indeed, the most fantastic, patriotic, and meaningful 4th of July they had ever heard of.

'Are you happy, my darling?' asked George, pulling Molly in tight as she sat beside him in the Cadillac.

'I couldn't be happier,' she told him.

It was true. George's ability to bring the glittering world of movies to her feet was surpassed only by his patriotism and passion for helping the less fortunate. The perfect husband. Molly couldn't help thinking that, after Tommy, a perfect husband was what she deserved.

She wasn't even dreading their wedding night, and that in itself was a huge testament to George's gentle nature. Molly held in her heart the secret wish that her honeymoon night would be perfect too. As perfect as her marriage. As perfect as George.

Chapter 11

Baubles, Bangles and Beads

You'll glitter and gleam so; make somebody dream, so that
Someday he may buy you a ring, ringa-linga
I've heard that's where it leads
Wearing baubles, bangles and beads

From Kismet, Robert Wright and George Forrest

George was very kind and loving to her in their wedding bed – everything that Tommy had failed to be - although he had a difficult time in fully consummating the marriage.

Though unsatisfied, Molly was pleased at his gentle lovemaking, for she knew that was what it was, and she showed a great deal of affection to George until they fell asleep in each other's arms.

They woke up early with their arms still wrapped around each other, and this time George was able to complete the marriage consummation. Afterwards, as they spent about an hour gently caressing and kissing each other, Molly attributed George's inability to stay aroused the previous night to wedding night nerves, or perhaps the champagne they'd had during their wedding day. She had noticed with Tommy that alcohol was a dual-edged sword: sometimes it made him want sex even though he blatantly had no real desire for her, and at other times it seemed to render him incapable. For those times, with Tommy, she'd been deeply grateful, and now she was grateful again as they helped her understand what might be going on.

They arose and dressed when they smelled the aroma of biscuits, bacon and coffee wafting up from the kitchen. They spent the day relaxing and carefully packing their suitcases for their two-week honeymoon trip through Canada. That night they enjoyed each other's company in bed, but once more George had some erection problems. Again, Molly showed nothing but kindness and understanding to George.

After a delicious and filling breakfast the next morning they departed for Niagara Falls, making one overnight stay on the way. They spent three full days in Niagara, enjoying the sight-seeing, fine restaurants, and shopping malls, then immersing themselves in the surrounding countryside and in the areas of Hamilton and Toronto. They then left for Prince Edward Island, with Molly fondly reliving her childhood memories of Anne of Green Gables, after passing through Montreal, Quebec, and Moncton with an overnight stay in each city. Next they drove to Halifax, Nova Scotia, then on to Yarmouth for the ferry ride over to Bar Harbor, Maine, where they stayed overnight in a rustic bed and breakfast inn. From there, they spent three days, with two overnight stays, driving to Molly's home arriving on Saturday night. They would then have Sunday to rest up before both going back to work on Monday.

It had been a wonderful, two-week honeymoon, marred only, for both, by George's recurring erectile dysfunction.

They attempted to make love every night of their trip, but George was successful in completing the act only five of the nights.

'That's what you get for marrying an old man,' George said glumly on more than one occasion.

'Not old, just older.' Molly kissed him gently. 'And we've got all the time in the world. This is only one part of a loving, married life, and I really, really couldn't ask for more.'

'And what about children? It seems like that might be a problem for me.'

Molly paused. No children with her first husband, and now maybe no children with her second husband? It wasn't really what she'd imagined - but then life had hardly worked out the way she'd imagined so far.

She reached for George's hand. 'How about we delay any plans for now, and then talk about it during our first year if we change our minds?'

'I think,' said George in a very relieved tone, 'that I just married the most wonderful woman in the world.'

They decided that they would both continue to work at their respective work sites, with George paying all their living expenses and Molly saving all, or most, of her pay checks as additional insurance for her future, if anything should happen to George. Molly already had a considerable amount saved from her income accrued since her divorce from Tommy.

George also revealed something that Molly had come to suspect: as the only child of his parents, he inherited their entire estate once they had both passed away, and was financially very well off.

Moreover, his inheritance was well invested, with a good rate of return, and he had added to it nearly every month from his income.

'We're very comfortable,' George confirmed as they totted up the household bills. 'We can – and should – indulge ourselves with frequent nights out, travel, and motorcycle riding. Even a two-week, honey-moon style vacation every year, to different places around the world.'

'If we could take my aunt and father with us occasionally, it would be perfect.'

'Your wish is my command,' said George with a smile.

They stayed for nearly two weeks in Molly's home before moving into a very nice apartment complex in a quaint, little, colonial-style village which was fairly close to George's workplace, and about the same distance to Molly's workplace as it was from her father's home. It was a beautifully furnished and decorated, maintenance-free, two-bedroom apartment with weekly maid service. It was located within walking distance of two fine restaurants, one of which served breakfast and lunch, and the other, lunch and dinner. Only a mile from a large grocery store, it was about the same distance away to the town square and the many shops and stores located there. Nearby was a beautiful park, shaded by many tall trees, mainly oaks and maples, and decorated with numerous flower gardens.

As soon as George parked the car on arrival to their new home on the first morning, he announced that he had a house-warming surprise for Molly. She immediately envisioned a house-hold appliance or a decorative art piece. However, instead of steering her into the apartment, after he parked their Cadillac in their expanded, three-car garage he led her to the far side of the garage. Next to his pick-up truck stood three motorcycles: his big Harley-Davidson, his classic Indian, and another custom-made and simply beautiful Indian - Molly's surprise wedding gift from her husband.

'I'll think of our wedding every time I ride it,' squealed Molly, falling instantly in love with it.

They then entered their new home, and walked around to admire the job that the decorators had done. It was a very beautiful, comfortable space. All the furniture was made of walnut, accented with beautiful, high-quality upholstery which, like the area rugs, lamps, linens and curtains were of high quality, in tonal, complementary colors. The walls of the living room, dining room, bathroom, and both bedrooms were hung with tasteful paintings, all with walnut frames gilded with gold. The spacious kitchen had walnut cabinets and pantry doors with beige stove and refrigerator, and other small appliances. They had everything they needed to embark on married life. After dressing for dinner, George drove them to the restaurant in their Cadillac, and they had excellent celebratory steak dinners.

They relaxed in their new home on Sunday, and organized their routine: rise at six am, bathe and dress for work, Molly would then make breakfast which she loved do to, drive themselves to work and then arrive home within half an hour of each other. They would have dinner out most evenings, enjoying the large variety of cuisine and atmosphere choices, and if they chose to stay home, Molly was an excellent maker of casseroles, and George was an expert on steak grilling and roast-baking.

On the evenings they had dinner at home, they often went for a walk in the town square area or around the walkways and paths of the park. There were frequent activities in and around the town square and park and plenty of time for them to enjoy them.

Thus began the general routine of their married life: going out most evenings for dinner; strolling about their little town and its parks at weekends; riding their motorcycles and taking a two-week vacation each year, either to various parts of their beautiful and wonderful country, or to other parts of the world. They frequently visited Jesse and Aunt Dolores, regularly attended motor cycle races, and occasionally saw friends and Molly's relatives, such as her sister Maureen, and her family. Most weeks, they had guests in their home, who often stayed overnight or even over the week-end.

It was a very busy, happy, socially-rich and adventuresome life, made all the more satisfying because they had practically no chores to do at home. On top of this, they both continued to advance in responsibilities and compensation in their employment.

Molly was very happy, living with George. He was a wonderful man who doted on her and lavished her with gifts and attention. Although he continued to have problems with love-making, this didn't bother her very much, and she took care never to show any disappointment to him, going out of her way to show her affection to him in bed and demonstrating her appreciation to him for the life style that he was providing for her. This was very easy for her to do, for George was always nice, genteel, courteous, respectful and loving to her. No one, not even her parents, had ever treated her better.

During the first few years of their marriage they visited Jesse and Aunt Dolores two or three times a month, but gradually their visits became less frequent, as they became more and more involved with their small-town lives. Unfortunately, during their seventh year of marriage, Aunt Dolores had a stroke, and within six months she had another one which caused her to be confined in a care facility. Because he was left alone in his large house, Jesse decided to retire from being County Sheriff at the end of his elective term, which was less than two years hence. During these times, George and Molly visited as often as they could, aiding Jesse with making decisions and plans for a retirement without Aunt Dolores, and helping him to make out his will.

Two months before Aunt Dolores was placed into the care of a nursing home, another tragedy occurred: Molly's brother-in-law, Angus, suddenly died of a heart attack. Fortunately for Maureen, three of her four sons were gone from the home - two of them married and raising families of their own, and the third one serving in the Navy. Only her youngest son was still living at home, and he was attending college part- time and working part-time. Angus was self-employed, and, therefore, did not have a retirement income, leaving Maureen with only a relatively small amount of life insurance. However, she also inherited Angus' half of their home, leaving her as the sole owner of the property.

At the time, Maureen was already helping her father, Molly and George to take care of Aunt Dolores, so it made sense all around that, as soon as Angus was buried and his will was probated, she should put her house up for sale and she and her son should move in with Jesse and Aunt Dolores. She was there to make nearly all of the arrangements for Aunt Dolores' move into the nursing home, and essentially replaced her in taking care of Jesse and the property. Maureen was still relatively young and seemingly in good health, so Molly was very pleased that she moved in with their father.

During the first four years of their marriage, George and Molly frequently rode their motorcycles, mostly on weekends when the weather was good, touring around the area within a 100-mile radius of their home. They visited scores of small towns within this area, walking around the courthouse squares, visiting antique and novelty stores, museums and other historic and natural history facilities, and enjoying meals in outstanding restaurants - especially those featuring "home cooking." Sometimes they ventured further from home to visit unique places, staying overnight in quaint hotels or small bed and breakfasts. Molly very much enjoyed these excursions and gradually became quite skilled in riding her Indian. They also attended six or more races a year. Try as she may, however, she never became enthusiastic about motorcycle races, unlike George, who remained as enamored as he had been for many years before marrying Molly.

After four years of marriage, George began to climb the corporate ladder. By their eighth year of marriage, he had been promoted to an executive vice president position, requiring him to make frequent out of town trips. He simply did not have the time to do many of the things they'd enjoyed during the earlier years of their marriage or the energy to do the things he did when he was younger. Quite frankly, Molly didn't mind. She did not miss the motorcycle riding, especially not going to the races.

In fact, she was beginning to feel that she could do without much of the frivolity that had characterized their early years together – though without it, she wasn't quite sure who they would be as a couple.

George was true to his word about traveling to interesting places of the world during a two-week vacation every year, and as promised, they often included Jesse and Aunt Dolores on the trips. At the start of their second year of marriage they took a two-week summer vacation to Arizona, Utah and Nevada. The third 'honeymoon' was divided into two parts. First, they treated Jesse and Aunt Dolores to a five-day Caribbean cruise, where they visited the Virgin Islands, Jamaica, Puerto Rico, and the Bahamas, and then they took a second cruise by themselves, spending two days in the Bahamas, and then visiting the Grand Caymans, Jamaica and the Dominican Republic, before ending up in Havana, Cuba.

As the cruise had been such a success, they repeated it during their third year. It became probably the greatest highlight of Jesse's and Aunt Dolores' lives. Later in the year, during the third week of October, the four of them took another cruise: five-days of cruising along the coasts of Massachusetts, New Hampshire, and Maine, with stops at Boston, Portsmouth and Bar Harbor and on into the Bay of Fundy, along the coasts of New Brunswick and Nova Scotia, with a final stop at Yarmouth. The cruise turned out to be extra special, because the foliage colorations of the forests that particular autumn was among the best in history.

They travelled the country far and wide, as well as visiting far-flung locations on cruises and organized tours. Molly often reminded herself how lucky she was in marrying such a wonderful man as George, who was also wealthy enough to allow them to take such wonderful vacations. Molly was especially excited about their seventh honeymoon: a two-week vacation in Hawaii, a place that she had always wanted to visit for a "romantic" vacation in a tropical paradise setting. It consisted of a round trip flight to Honolulu; a tour of Oahu; and a cruise around the five major islands of: Hawaii, Maui, Molokai, Oahu and Kauai.

They arrived at Honolulu airport in the early afternoon on Sunday, and after being greeted Hawaiian-style, they picked up their rental car and drove to the Hyatt Hotel on Waikiki Beach, from where they would spend five days touring Oahu before boarding their cruise ship. They started their visits on Oahu by driving around the periphery of the island, stopping in Haleiwa for lunch and in Kaneolie for dinner, returning to the hotel for an evening entertainment of hula dancing and singing. After breakfast at the hotel the next morning they left to tour some of the island's military monuments: the USS Arizona Memorial at Pearl Harbor; the Punchbowl National Memorial Cemetery of the Pacific, and the defensive big gun installations on Diamond Head. Their third day was spent in visiting military museums at Pearl Harbor, Schofield Barracks, Hickam Airforce Base, Wheeler Airforce Base, and Fort Kamehameha; arriving back at the hotel in time to attend a luau, with typical native foods and entertainment. They decided to spend their entire fourth day at the Polynesian Cultural Center, at Laie - the Mormon

Church's elaborate and beautiful center which celebrates the many cultures of Polynesia.

They were amazed to read that nearly all the Polynesians who worked and/or performed at the Center were members of the Mormon church, and were attending the university across the road from the Center. The university was a branch of Brigham Young University. At the time, the campus was in an active building phase, so most, of the buildings in use, were temporary wooden structures, scattered over the developing campus of 400 acres. The temporary wooden structures were gradually being replaced by permanent brick and stone buildings (one was nearly completed and three more were under construction). The central road went from the Center, through the middle of the campus for approximately two miles, where it terminated at a very large, magnificent, Mormon Temple. Interestingly, the university and Center operated as a student/faculty cooperative, like that of venerable Berea College in south-central Kentucky.

They had planned on driving around the western half of the island during the fifth day, but changed their minds and revisited the Center and the Punch Bowl cemetery. At the cemetery, they were indelibly impressed by the incredible cost to the nation of defeating the Japanese in the Pacific theater of war, and then at the Center they spent most of their time seeing native dance and ritual performance, talking with as many of the performers as they could. Of the many Polynesian cultures represented, they were most impressed with the Maoris, Samoans and Tongans. They were very impressed with how tall the people were, especially the well-built and light-skinned Maoris and the huge, stout Samoans.

Before leaving, they purchased most of the books and booklets, and a few souvenirs, from several of the gift shops. They left the Center with a tremendous admiration of the Polynesian people, as well as with a great respect for the Mormon church.

Early the next morning, they checked out of the hotel, dropped off their rental car near where their cruise ship was berthed, and embarked into the ship, and were immediately escorted to their "cabin." It was a comfortable well-appointed, two-room suite, with a large bathroom and a large balcony, and furnished with two chairs, two lounges and two side tables. George had arranged for one of the best suites on the ship, without Molly's knowledge, as a surprise to her.

After unpacking their luggage and stowing their clothing and other things in the dresser drawers and cabinets, they had several glasses of champagne, toasting the beginning of their romantic cruise around the islands. Then they took a stroll around the ship, sampling some of the gourmet fare before cleaning up and changing into formal attire for dinner. After a delicious gourmet dinner, of which they both ate too much, they strolled over to the ship's main theater to watch the featured stage shows of the evening. There were several very entertaining short shows followed by a highly professional two-hour stage production featuring dancing and singing entertainers dressed in elaborate, colorful costumes.

Finally, they retired to their suite and sat for up to a half hour on their private balcony, chatting about the events of the day and speculating on the coming days events. Before arising in the morning, they would lazily make love. They would then clean up in the bathroom, dress casually and then debark at the morning's port of call.

This would be their basic everyday routine over the week-long cruise. Unfortunately, George was frustrated with his inability to sexually satisfy Molly or himself during their love-making sessions. As usual, Molly made sure not to show any disappointment, instead making sure that she demonstrated her love, happiness and respect for her husband.

She was becoming increasingly aware, however, that for her, the problem with their marriage was not the physical issue. Rather, it was the lack of anything more normal, more substantial – children, the satisfaction of cooking a wonderful meal or growing crops on the land. It was all too shiny, and, if she was honest, too easy.

After the cruise, George and Molly took a direct flight home to the Pittsburg Airport, arriving late Sunday afternoon. The trip back was tiring, so they didn't bother to completely unpack. Instead they drove to their favorite restaurant for a quick dinner, so that they could get to bed early to get as much rest as possible before going back to work on Monday morning. They easily slipped back into their work routines, and ate out most evenings over the next few weeks, with little other activity.

Molly still visited Aunt Dolores as often as she could, and George went with her when his work schedule allowed. They tried to encourage her recovery and cheer her up by planning to take her and Jesse on further trips. However, with each visit they noticed that her health was rapidly deteriorating, until two weeks after Easter, she passed away.

As summer approached they asked Jesse if he would like to go on the cruise, even though Aunt Dolores was gone, and perhaps to take Maureen along if she wanted to come with them; but he declined. Able to please themselves entirely, they decided to scrap the cruise in favour of a cross-country train trip to spend a week vacation in Yellowstone Park.

The total time it took for the train-trip to the park was approximately six days, with the highlight being the very spectacular scenery they enjoyed passing through Glacier National Park. The bus dropped them off at the famous Lake Yellowstone Hotel, where they had reservations for four nights. This venerable hotel, which was built in 1891, had very comfortable, spacious, rustic, rooms, which were beautifully decorated. Moreover, it had a huge, beautiful dining room and several cafes and bars. On the morning after their fourth night at the Lake Yellowstone Hotel, they transferred to the even more famous Old Faithful Inn, a sprawling hotel which was built in 1903 near to the Old Faithful geyser. The scenery was unbelievably spectacular, and they felt quite fortunate to have been able to visit this most spectacular and vast national park.

They arrived home full of stories and memories. Jesse drove them to one of his favorite restaurants which featured "down-home cookin'", and both Jesse and Maureen were rapt as they listened to George and Molly describe their vacation, especially as neither of them had ever ridden on a train, let alone spent several nights on one.

'It was wonderful,' said Molly enthusiastically. 'You should definitely try it.'

She saw Maureen cast a glance in her direction, then her sister said, 'I need to freshen up. Molly, keep me company?'

In the bathroom, Maureen asked her sister, in a low, sympathetic voice: 'What's going on with you? Did you not enjoy your vacation?'

'Of course I did!' said Molly, stunned. 'Did you not hear everything we were just saying? It was wonderful! You should definitely try it.'

'There!' cried Maureen triumphantly. 'That's about the fourth time you've said that, like you didn't really think it was wonderful at all.'

Molly applied her lipstick, not quite sure what to say.

'I think there are only so many wonderful adventures you can have in one lifetime, Maureen,' she said with a sigh, 'before they all become a little … empty.'

Maureen didn't reply, but simply rubbed her sister's back in great sympathy.

With a sinking heart, Molly noticed that it was exactly the same thing she had done to Maureen when Angus died.

As the couple struggled with their marriage, and began to noticeably drift apart, they looked for ways to recover the carefree happiness they had enjoyed during the first seven years together. They took pains to plan a very special honeymoon vacation for the start of their ninth year of marriage. Their decision was to take the romantic river cruise in Europe that they had been promising themselves for years, cruising to London on the Big U, catching a ferry across the English Channel to Amsterdam, taking an exciting train ride to Amsterdam and a Rhine River cruise back to

Amsterdam; and then a ferry toward the white cliffs of Dover, back to London, where they boarded the Big U for the cruise back to New York.

Both George and Molly agreed that it was an amazing, enjoyable, and jam-packed vacation, highlighted by visiting parts of Europe that had been war-torn and ravaged - like Cologne Cathedral and the bridges along the Rhine.

For George, the only thing which spoiled the trip for him was his inability to make proper love to his lovely wife. He failed every night of the trip, and even though Molly was very understanding, and showed not a bit of disappointment in his failure, he was, nevertheless, highly disappointed in himself.

For Molly, it seemed that their years were simply blending into one, punctuated only by sad events in their families and the next cruise or holiday that they'd booked.

After the Europe cruise, they went over to visit with Jesse and Maureen and go through the annual ritual of sharing the details of their vacation with them. However, it simply was not the same with Aunt Dolores missing.

It simply wasn't the same any more, period.

Her marriage was adrift, and they both knew it.

And so did the man at work – the one who had fallen in love with her.

As much as it broke her heart, Molly knew that she couldn't stay married to George. Despite everything they shared, it was no longer enough. It was her soul that needed love and vacations, not her body.

Chapter 12

Love at first sight

You looked very beautiful tonight standing by the store room door.
After you left, Danny asked me who the pretty girl was.
I told him just a friend.
I'd like to tell them all that you are my one and only.

Charlie's first love letter

He was helplessly smitten in an instant. He didn't even know who she was, although she obviously worked in the factory. She simply came to the window of the tool and stock room, where he had worked for the past six months, to requisition a box of pencils.

He took the requisition slip from her in a daze, his hand trembling.

The woman began to flush under the intensity of his gaze, so he tore his eyes away from her and forced himself to look at the slip. Pencils. Pencils. Think of something to say about pencils, he told himself. But she seemed to have taken away his power of speech.

He found the box he needed instantly and yet he still leaned against the shelf for a moment, pretending he was still searching. What was happening to him? This was a woman he had never seen before. He didn't even know her name. And how could he even find it out? She was dressed in typical factory attire, including the usual smock worn by the female employees, and while she was very attractive and seemed to be about his age, he wasn't sure how that description was going to help him in a factory employing dozens of women. "Attractive and about my age" could apply to many of them.

When he could sustain his fake search no longer, he returned to the window and slid the box across to her, signing the requisition slip at the same time.

'Don't use them all at once,' he said in an attempt at a joke, but even as the words were leaving his lips he chastised himself. She *should* use them all at once. Then she'd have to come back.

'I promise,' said the woman solemnly, but her eyes were twinkling above freckled cheeks that were still tinged with pink. 'Bye.'

Too soon she was gone, leaving her impression imprinted eternally on Charlie's heart.

Her smile was devastatingly beautiful. Charlie was so flustered that he hadn't even thought to introduce himself, or find out her name. Feeling foolish, he realised that he could easily have made her sign the requisition slip too. He could have made something up. Instead he had let her slip through his fingers, and he began to panic, thinking that he might never see her again. That, too, was highly unlikely, as all employees visited the stock room from time to time, but deep down he was aware that he wasn't prepared to leave it to chance.

He had to see her again.

Charlie knew that this was the proverbial 'love at first sight'. He'd read a few novels in the prison library, and from how it was apparently meant to feel, he knew this was it: a pounding heart, a tunnelling of time and space, a feeling that the other half of his soul had just walked away with a carton of pencils.

And yet, how was that possible? He was a married man with three small children, and a fourth on the way – and not just a married man, but a happily married man. Wasn't he? He was certainly still content in his married life, and there had never been any serious problems during nearly three years of marriage.

On the other hand, he had essentially no experience with romantic love, having married a very young Muriel immediately after being released from a twenty-year period of monastic life in prison, at the age of thirty-five. He had known family love before – and during – his incarceration, but prison was practically devoid of love apart from the bond of brotherhood that had bound them together as inmates, and, of course, his enduring devotion to God. His only connection to romantic love was what he'd read about in the prison library, and what he believed he'd felt for Muriel. Of late, he'd become increasingly aware that they might even have been falling short of Muriel's own fantasies about what married life might be like, but he'd never for a moment imagined himself wanting to break his marriage vows.

But this? This was a compulsion, as if he were being propelled into extraordinary actions by a chance meeting with the love of his life.

If Charlie knew anything more than any other man, it was how the chance meetings in life could have astonishing results on what happened to a person. The last time, it had led to unimaginable horror.

This time, it could lead to a life-long passion, the coming together of a dream that he hadn't even know he had. He had to do something.

The moment he had a break in the day, Charlie shot up the stairs toward the payroll office. Amos and he were still such very close friends, laughing frequently, that they seem to have swapped their neighboring cells for neighboring offices.

As ever, Amos was peering through his round spectacles, studying a list of figures and jabbing at the counting machine. He was far better at mental arithmetic, but always liked to have the sheet of paper typed out with all his calculations so that he could justify and demonstrate the factory's wage payments. 'I'm never going to be called a thief again, Charlie,' he'd said to his friend when he'd first started, and he made sure he had paper trails that would have kept McCarthy happy.

He held a hand up to Charlie, entered a couple more numbers, and then relaxed with a smile. 'Charlie boy,' he said. 'Is it lunchtime again? I'm sure I wasn't here all night, but you never can tell …'

'No, not lunchtime. I'm feeding my heart, not my stomach.' Charlie closed the door behind him. 'I need you to tell me someone's name.'

'For the new baby?' said Amos, puzzled.

Charlie's mouth went dry. This was not the time to be thinking of the new baby – or rather, with a fourth child on the way, this was not the time to be tracking down female colleagues. But he couldn't help himself. Furthermore, he knew that Amos would understand this must be something very important to him. He'd known him for years, better than anyone, and the last thing Charlie could ever be was an uncaring philanderer.

'I don't know how to say this, Amos, but I ... I think I've fallen in love.'

Amos leaned back in his chair. 'You're a married man, Charlie. A very married man.'

'I know,' said Charlie, 'and I would never set out to hurt Muriel, but I can't help myself. I ... I just met her; I don't even know her name, and yet I am convinced that this is the woman I'm meant to spend the rest of my life with.'

'And she works here in the factory?'

Charlie nodded. For several moments, Amos fiddled with his spectacles and stared at Charlie, and he felt exactly as he always had standing before Warden Kelly, waiting for some great pronouncement.

Then Amos sighed. 'All right. Most folks who work here have turned up in the office at some time or other, asking about their wages. I might be able to identify her. But I'm only giving you her name, okay? I don't want to be party to anything underhanded.'

'I understand. Thank you, Amos.' Charlie could feel his chest flooding with heat. 'Okay, so she's ... she's an exceptionally lovely woman. Taller than most women, really quite tall, and slender as a stem of wheat. She has reddish-blonde hair like a harvest sunset, a heart-warming smile, and the voice of an angel.'

Amos rolled his eyes. 'You really have fallen in love, haven't you?'

'Do you know who she is?'

'I think so.' Amos wrote a name on a blank wage slip, and handed it to his friend. 'I think it's the requisition clerk.'

'Yes! She came to me for pencils.'

Amos laughed softly. 'Well, there you have it, my friend. That's her name. The rest is up to you.'

Charlie left the payroll office in a dream, staring at the name on the chit. Molly Goodwin. Molly. What a lovely name, he thought, his heart leaping with joy even at knowing such paltry information such as her name and where she worked. It made sense that she would have a lovely name. It would be even lovelier, he thought, if it was combined with his surname.

It seemed like complete madness. A moment of craziness that could end disastrously. But Charlie knew that he couldn't stop himself. Some force of nature had taken over, and now he and Molly were riding that wave toward an uncertain future, no matter what happened.

He waited until she appeared again at the stock room door before making any kind of move, and in the few days before he saw her again he did everything he could to persuade himself away from the course of action that seemed to be opening up for him. Amos did the same, reminding Charlie again and again that Muriel was a wonderful wife, and a great mother to their children. Charlie couldn't and didn't disagree, but his heart was leading the way, and it held an unstoppable momentum.

'Hi, Charlie. I need some requisition forms, please.'

Hearing her voice at the stock room window, Charlie forced himself to stay calm and smile agreeably. She'd used his name. He hadn't told her what it was, so she must have gone to some effort to find it out. He couldn't believe how pleased he was that she used his name when she greeted him.

'Certainly. It's Molly, isn't it? I'll just get those for you. Molly.' Now he was using her name as often as possible, just for the pleasure of hearing how it sounded on his lips.

Again, she offered him that beautiful smile. 'Thank you, Charlie.'

He filled her order as slowly as possible, and then sidled past his desk as she was assembling the pile of goods. Just as she was ready to leave, he handed her the note that he'd taken from his drawer – a note that had been prepared for just this occasion, from the moment he'd discovered her name.

She reached out to take it, and for the first time Charlie noticed that she wore a ring on her left hand. A wedding ring. For some reason, he had not thought about the possibility that she was married, and he almost snatched back the note. As he went to grab it again their fingers touched, and a sensation like an electric shock charged through his hand. They both gasped and let go, and then Molly stared at the note, looked back at Charlie, and deliberately drew it toward her.

'Thank you, Charlie,' she said again, so quietly that he could hardly hear her, and then she left.

He waited until the click of her heels had disappeared down the stairway before sinking into his chair. What had he done? They were both married! And they worked together, which was bound to cause some difficulties, and he might, in any case, have completely mis-read the situation.

Of course, he reasoned, it might actually help his cause that she was also married. If she was *happily* married, then she would automatically spurn his advances, and that would be that. On the other hand, her situation might be similar to his, which was something Charlie had only realised when he'd laid eyes on Molly the week before. The situation with him and Muriel was that he wasn't unhappily married, but he wasn't truly happily married either - simply because he hadn't truly known what love really was.

Charlie recalled what he'd said in his note as he wrote it on one side of a piece of lined paper from a small writing tablet, and wondered how Molly would feel reading it.

Dearest Molly,

Forgive me if I seem impertinent or insult you in any way. That is the furthest thing from my heart.

The thing is, I had never experienced true love until I saw you at the store room the other day, and I fear that if I don't tell you how I feel that we may never be together in the way that I know we are meant to be – that is, forever, completely and always.

If you feel even slightly the same way, then please agree to meet with me. We can go somewhere innocent and open, like the cafeteria, and it will be enough for me. Enough to dare to hope that you might feel like me, even if it's just in a small way for now.

Your friend, Charlie.'

Had he gone too far? He might be the laughing stock of the requisition office by now, or even the whole factory.

But then she answered his note in only a few hours – discreetly and amiably. A woman from Molly's office stopped by to invite him to sit at her table for lunch.

Oh, and Molly would be there too.

Charlie was pleasantly stunned. She had responded quickly, and the answer was positive. His mind began racing with romantic fantasies. In less than an hour they would have their first "date". They would soon begin getting to know each other. There would be a whirlwind courtship, and before long a marriage, and they would live happily ever after. Suddenly, Charlie was happier than he had ever been in his life. He was in love!

And any thoughts of difficulty did not belong in the mind and heart of a man in love. This was truly special, and as something so heart-felt had to be sent from Heaven, Charlie knew that their love would be supported. He would look for signs, and if any seemed to indicate that this was not the avenue he was meant to walk along, with his soul-mate, then he would take heed. But he hoped fervently that all would go well. It was time to be deeply happy.

Chapter 13

An Order of Love

Date: ANY TIME
Charge Account No.: US
To Be Used For: LOVE
Job Order No.: OURS
Quantity Ordered: EVERY BIT
Description: LOVE IN EVERY WAY
Quantity Delivered: ALL, LITTLE BY LITTLE
Approved By: YOU AND ME
Received By: BOTH OF US

Molly's love requisition form

To begin with, Molly was completely taken aback by the sudden attention paid to her by the handsome, sandy-haired man working in the factory supply and tool room.

She had worked at the factory for the past twelve years, but only recently did her job require her to visit the supply room periodically, usually to pick up office supplies, or the regulation smocks the ladies needed to wear over their street clothing. The supply room dispensed nearly every item needed by the factory workers to do their jobs, mostly tools and metal parts, and there were several men working there during each of the factory's shifts. She had noticed him, of course, on earlier occasions, but she'd always been served by someone else – usually Danny, who had a roguish twinkle in his eye but seemed generally harmless.

Charlie, however, was another matter. He didn't flirt like Danny, or banter with her like many of the other men who worked at the factory. He was somehow more serious, more intense, and his attempts to make her laugh seemed clumsy. Even the way he avoided looking at her caused her to blush, because she could tell that he was forcing himself to avert his gaze, as if she were a bright light that might sear his vision. She also wondered if he did that deliberately to make her less uncomfortable, because there could be no doubt that his presence affected her.

He was lingering over her orders, she could tell, becoming more friendly and talkative. And then it happened. As she reached to pick up her order, his hand touched hers and the effect was electric. She was sure that she blushed, and that he noticed it.

Molly had scurried away the first time, angry with herself for feeling an attraction to the man. After all, she was a married woman and had always lived by a strict moral code. She had never considered walking out with another man throughout either of her marriages, even though many had hinted at it and despite the fact that nobody would have judged her for it during her time with Tommy.

Even with George, while she had come to realise that she wasn't genuinely happy and that all the possessions and luxuries in the world couldn't fill the ache in her soul, she would never have countenanced breaking her vows. George was a good man and a loving husband, and he didn't deserve that.

When she found out that Charlie was married – with three children by his very young wife, according to Annette who worked part-time in the payroll office with Amos, Charlie's friend – that settled the matter. Under no circumstances would she even consider going out with him, now that she knew he had children. She herself had never been blessed with offspring, and it seemed unlikely now that she ever would, but she could not imagine any parent wanting to disrupt their children's lives in any way. She had only her own parents' marriage as her guiding light, and she knew that her father would disown her if she were to interfere in another marriage in which children were involved. Living by the Ten Commandments and the Golden Rule, he called it, even though he was not particularly religious.

And yet she had to admit that there was something about Charlie. Occasionally she would catch one of his unguarded glances; they sent shockwaves through her, and she began to avoid going to the supply room in case she felt her resistance lowering.

'He's mighty handsome,' Annette would say with a wink when she caught her friend trying not to watch him across the cafeteria.

'I'm sure his wife thinks so too,' was Molly's firm reply.

She was determined, then, that nothing would happen. But then one morning, a few days after she'd first spoken to him at the supply room, Annette caught her by the arm and dragged her out of the food queue to the small area where the trays were stacked.

'You have to hear this,' Annette hissed from behind at tray tower. 'Dolly, the cleaning lady, was going around the offices collecting crockery the other day when she overheard a conversation in the next office, and it was about you!'

'Was it the supply office? Because if it was, I don't want to hear about that man having lewd fantasies about me. We are both married,' she said primly.

But Annette leaned in closer. 'No, it was my office! The payroll office, and Charlie was talking to Amos.'

'About me?'

'Yes, and oh, Molly,' said Annette, clutching her hands to her bosom, 'he's completely, head-over-heels in love with you!'

Molly stared at her, her pulse ticking in her throat. She could feel her skin flushing to her hairline. Love? That wasn't possible, was it?

'It doesn't change anything.' Molly shook her head as if shaking the fanciful notions of love out of her head. 'We're both happily married.'

Annette cocked her head on one side. 'Really? I mean, don't take this the wrong way, but you don't really seem that happy lately. And as for Charlie — well, did you ever hear of a man declaring himself in love before he's even kissed the girl? That man is not as happily married as anyone thinks. Not like he'd be,' and she gave Molly with a mischievous nudge, 'married to you.'

'You're crazy,' laughed Molly.

'No, he's crazy. Crazy in love.'

Molly watched Annette sauntering away, holding her tray aloft as she swished her way through the tables. What did she know? Nobody could explain what being in love felt like.

But suddenly Molly realised that she couldn't either. She'd never been in love. For sure, she loved and admired George. But this feeling, the sense of two parts making a whole, creating electricity – well, that was something she had only experienced with one man, across a counter, holding a box of pencils.

She left it a couple of days just to be sure that she was really feeling the beginning of a genuine and pure emotion. For nothing less would she consider hurting George. Then, when her heart urged her to press forward, she invented a list of items and approached the supply room.

He was reading through a stock-sheet at his desk, so she called out to him. His delight at her arrival was palpable, and he spoke her name aloud as if it were the most delicious thing he'd ever tasted. Electricity had passed through their fingers again as they touched.

And he passed her something – a note, a personal note – with such hope and anguish in his eyes that she couldn't help but know that his intentions were true, and that this train had already left the station.

Their first conversation was at the lunch table, with Annette talking more than either of them. They met again in the cafeteria, not every day so that people commented, but often enough to be able to talk and share stories. To begin to know each other. The notes continued to come regularly, handed to her at the supply office or passed on to her by her willing accomplice, Annette, and in time she began to respond, replying on requisition notes or order forms or whatever paper she had to hand.

Finally, they dared to meet outside the cafeteria. Avoiding evenings where they might get too caught up in their emotions, Charlie took her to a little restaurant not too far from the factory. It was so simple compared with the lavish settings in which she and George dined that Molly was a little taken aback, but it was charming and quiet, and that was what Charlie had wanted more than anything.

They ordered quickly, and then leaned toward each other across the table as if magnetized, Molly aware of the warmth of Charlie's knee against her own.

'I'm so glad you're here,' said Charlie with his usual intense gaze. 'I can hardly believe it.'

'It's probably against my better judgment.' Molly toyed with her napkin, more nervous than she cared to admit. 'But I'm happy we're here too.'

Charlie reached out his hand. 'There are ... I want to tell you some things. I know they may change this, and whatever you may feel about it, but I have to be completely honest with you if we have any chance of being together properly.'

'Okay,' said Molly hesitantly. 'Is this about you being married? Because I already know that.'

'It's about ...' Charlie didn't seem to know quite where to start. 'Well, before I got married, I was ... I was in prison. For twenty years,' he blurted. 'I was involved in a bank robbery at the age of fifteen, and I was only meant to be the driver so I really didn't know what I was getting into. Anyway, it was a blood bath, and fifteen people died including some law-enforcement officers and some innocent bystanders. I was spared from the chair because of my age and so on, but sentenced to life imprisonment. I was paroled after two decades when they changed the regulations for lifers, particularly those with exemplary records.'

He looked at Molly with fear in his eyes, then paused for the waiter to put down their plates.

'Would you say something?'

She hardly knew where to start. 'Did ... did you—' She couldn't bring herself to use the word "kill", 'hurt anyone?'

'Not a soul,' said Charlie earnestly. 'I couldn't hurt a fly, and I would never hurt a human being, least of all you.'

'And you didn't know what you were doing?'

Charlie placed his hand over his heart. 'I swear on the lives of my babies that I did not know what I was involved in.'

Molly could see how serious he was. 'I don't really know what to say, but ... thank you for telling me.'

'That's not all I wanted to tell you, though, Molly,' said Charlie, his eyes haunted as if he was plowing on through this fears. 'I got married straight out of prison. Muriel's much younger than me, and, you know, very fertile.'

'You've got three children.'

Charlie nodded, then sighed. 'And another on the way. The baby's due in a few months.'

'Another? Muriel's pregnant – right now?'

Charlie bowed his head miserably. 'I know how it sounds, Molly, but it doesn't change a single iota of how I feel about you.'

Molly's chest heaved with the effort of holding down her emotion, of not getting upset in the middle of a restaurant. She had believed that he might love her, that he might be unhappy in his marriage as she was recognizing herself to be, but this told a different story. He was still having relations with Muriel. He was a family man, with people relying on him. He had a young wife, young children, a baby about to come into the world …

She stood quickly, scraping back her chair. 'I have to go.'

'But your food …'

'I'm not hungry,' she said, unable to disguise her bitterness.

She left the café abruptly, hearing Charlie call her name and run after her. In the parking lot, he caught up with her.

'I'm so sorry, Molly. I didn't want to upset you. But I mean it – it doesn't change how I feel about you.'

Molly shook her head. 'But it changes how I feel about you.'

'No, please don't tell me that,' he said, trying to pull her toward him.

She shook herself out of his embrace. 'Please take me back to the factory,' she said stiffly. 'And once we're there, I think it will be better if we don't see each other again.'

They drove back in silence, Charlie's jaw set in a grim right angle as Molly tried to drown out the sound of her own heart splitting into little pieces. It was not to be. It could never have been. What had she been thinking?

Chapter 14

Never a Gambling Man

You have got to help me keep a level head. I love you so much, but I know I have a responsibility and you have a greater one than I ... Honey, you have got to stay and raise those children up or until they are old enough to understand what we have.

Molly's letter to Charlie

Charlie was devastated that his honesty had put Molly off so completely. He'd known that he had to tell her the truth, or he wouldn't be able to live with himself, but he hadn't anticipated her reaction.

For days, he didn't see her, and she refused to respond to any requests to see him, via note or Annette and any other way he could think of. However, he knew she would have to come to the store room at some point, so he wrote his next note in advance of her arrival, and placed it under a pad on his workstation ready to slide across to her.

Sure enough, one day she turned up at the store room door, trying not to catch his eye. Danny stood up to deal with her request, and Molly looked almost grateful that she wouldn't have to talk to Charlie.

She was just about to depart, her arms loaded with goods, when Charlie slipped across to her. On top of her pile of stationery, he added a book of order forms with his note cushioned between its pages. 'I think you forgot this,' he said quietly.

'Oh, sorry – did I leave something off your list?' Danny was about to walk over and inspect the order form again.

'No, that's fine,' said Molly, retreating quickly into the corridor.

Charlie's heart leapt. She wasn't rejecting his note – not at this point, anyway. 'It's just that thing I forgot last time,' he said with a smile, trying to look business-like.

'Of course.'

She was gone again before Charlie could say any more.

Danny had watched the exchange with a raised eyebrow. Now he just nodded to Charlie, hiding a faint smile, and tucked his pencil back behind his ear. 'Just a friend, huh?'

'Maybe not even that,' Charlie replied. 'But maybe more. Much more.'

The note that Molly was (hopefully) about to read was full of apologies for upsetting her, and then went on to suggest that Molly and her husband, George, came to his home on Saturday to play cards with himself and Muriel.

"If I can't have you to myself,' the note explained, 'then I have to find some way to be with you as friends. There is something special between us, Molly, and even if that is just friendship, then I'd like to preserve that. It will just be two old married couples, doing what old married couples do.'

To his great relief and excitement, Molly agreed, and so that Saturday Molly arrived with her husband at his home.

Charlie shook George's hand with a feeling of trepidation. This was the husband of the woman he loved, coming into his home to play cards with Charlie and the woman he was meant to be in love with. It didn't make sense, but somehow Charlie really liked George. He was older than Molly, more fatherly than he'd expected. Molly was greeting Muriel with equal pleasantness, and he could see that she, too, was startled to be confronted with the age difference between himself and Muriel.

'This is so nice!' cried Muriel, clapping her hands excitedly. 'I'm so fond of cards, so imagine my delight when Charlie told me that you'd chatted about your favorite games at the factory.'

'She almost forced me to ask you over,' said Charlie, barely able to take his eyes off Molly, strikingly dressed as she was in a brocade dress which highlighted her tall, slender figure. He forced himself to look at George. 'And Molly told me you're quite the canasta king.'

George smiled pleasantly. 'Well, we've had the good fortune to play cards in some of the finest casinos in the world, haven't we, Molly?'

Molly appeared embarrassed, and after a quick, 'Oh, I don't know,' she concentrated on talking to Betty, who was looking after the children while the card games went on.

'Monaco, Paris, we've been to so many it's hard to recall,' continued George.

Muriel squealed. 'Oh, Paris! I can't believe you've visited all these amazing places. Was the fashion simply the most?'

'The most what?' said George, genuinely puzzled.

Charlie tried not to laugh. It was like a grandpa talking to his young granddaughter, and here were Molly and himself, both in their late thirties, stuck in the middle with everything in common and no way to express it.

He watched her now as she met his children, her hand across her chest as she smiled wistfully at three-year old Detty and the twins who were now a year old.

'Are you hoping for a boy so that you have two of each?' she asked Muriel carefully.

'Boy, girl, I don't really care. I'm just hoping for it to be over soon,' said Muriel, forcing a laugh. 'I can't wait to be able to fit into a dress like yours, Molly. It's simply divine!'

'Thank you, Muriel. And thank you again for having us here, it really is kind of you.'

Muriel shooed her mother and the children out of the room. 'It's my pleasure, believe me. An evening having fun with friends and no children around – why, it's exactly what someone my age should be doing!'

Charlie exchanged helpless glances with Molly, as Muriel passed around the drinks and George dealt out the cards, and in that moment, he knew that she felt exactly the same way. Her expression said it all: that she'd be delighted to be here in this happy home with Charlie, sitting quietly with a child or two on their laps and talking as the setting sun disappeared over the horizon. She had no more wish to be gallivanting around to exotic places with George than he desired to be out jiving with Muriel and her friends. This was perfect – playing cards, wonderful conversation, loving family around. Perfect. Or at least it would be, if it was just the two of them.

And Charlie knew that the next time they met, it had to be just that. The two of them, alone together. The evening passed pleasantly enough, but all it did for Charlie was increase his passion for Molly, because he could see what they could have together, and it wasn't what they had right now. Not unhappily married, but not truly happy either. And what was life about, if it wasn't about being happy? He felt terrible for being in the slightest bit untrue to Muriel, and knew that Molly felt the same way too, but he had to see where this was going. He had to find out more.

The next note he passed to Molly was inviting her to go to a highly-advertised John Wayne movie with him the following weekend.

She appeared at the stock room window, checking that Danny wasn't there before waving the note at him. 'Do you mean with George and Muriel?'

'No.' Charlie chose his words carefully, remembering what his overt honesty had achieved before. 'No, I mean the two of us, on our own, at the movies like … like sweethearts.'

Molly sighed. 'I don't know, Charlie. I think if we take our spouses we can at least pretend that we don't have these feelings for each other.'

'I don't want to pretend,' said Charlie simply.

'I'll think about it.' Molly said it in such a way that Charlie knew she meant she'd be thinking about everything, not just the movie – where this was headed, how she felt about him, all of it. Because now she'd admitted it. She did have feelings for him.

'I'll only go if George doesn't need me, or have plans for the two of us.'

It was sweet, really, that she still put George first. 'I understand,' said Charlie, and he truly did.

As it turned out, George had scheduled some work at the plant so Molly could get away. They met outside the movie theater as breathless as teenagers.

'I can't believe I'm doing this,' said Molly.

Charlie grinned. 'I can't believe I've waited all my life to do this,' he said.

'I need to be home by five.' Molly scanned the street anxiously, clearly worried that someone might recognise her. 'Let's go inside.'

He bought tickets to the early afternoon of the latest John Wayne film, "The Sea Chase". Holding two boxes of popcorn and a bag of Bit O'Honey candy, he escorted her to a seat in the middle of the theater. The thrill of sitting beside her was acute, accompanied by the sweet pain of knowing that something so ordinary and straightforward was, for them, forbidden.

After a Movie-Tone newsreel, a Loony Tunes cartoon and previews of the upcoming movies, the main feature began. Finishing his popcorn, Charlie laid his arm along the top of her seat, as if it was the most natural thing in the world. He waited for an exciting section in the film to drop his arm down to Molly's shoulders.

At first, she acted as if she was unaware of his arm, focusing her attention on the screen. At a dramatic moment, Charlie clasped Molly's shoulder. Instinctively, it seemed, Molly laid her head against Charlie's shoulder and he pulled her comfortably toward him. Molly glanced up at him, red-cheeked, but made no attempt to move, and they stayed in this position until the end of the show. When the lights came on, Charlie helped her from her seat and continued holding her hand as he accompanied her to her car.

The parking lot was quiet as all the shoppers had vacated town. Charlie could feel the electricity from their joined hands surging around his body, and he knew without doubt that he had never experienced love like this before.

Molly opened the car door. 'Thank you, Charlie,' she said quietly, staring at his lapel. 'I had … the most wonderful time.'

It was the sign he needed. She meant the most wonderful time she'd ever had.

He couldn't help himself. Putting his arm around her waist, he drew her toward him and kissed her gently. He felt Molly's body stiffen and then relax, and suddenly she was kissing him back.

It was only brief, but the powerful undercurrent of passion was something that would remain with Charlie for the rest of his life – a life that would have to, somehow, be with Molly.

For the next month or so, the letter writing continued at work. Charlie was aware that his notes were becoming longer and more ardent, inspired by the fact that Molly began to answer them more frequently, albeit with short responses.

They also carried on playing card games with George and Muriel, alternating between Molly's home and Charlie's. Muriel was pleased with these get-togethers – she obviously liked the other couple and enjoyed any excuse to forget that she was a young mother of nearly four children – and George seemed to be reserved but tolerant about them. It was as if Charlie and Molly could convince themselves that they were not in love with each other, as long as they had the counter-balances of their respective spouses involved.

Outside the factory or the card-games, however, they would have lunch together in a nearby café or restaurant then end with a quick kiss before returning to work, or sometimes park in a secluded street and pour out their passion for each other in snatched moments.

They stopped having lunch together in the factory lunchroom, thinking that it was best that they not be seen together too often.

Molly, in particular, was careful to ensure that their conversations were not overheard, and that they weren't appearing too "friendly" to their co-workers.

Before too long, it became clear that they couldn't carry on like this. They both wanted more – more time together, more intimacy, more honesty in the expression of their love – and being married to different people, no matter how wonderful they were in their own way, was not the way ahead.

Chapter 15

The Sinner

Princess, your love and kisses seem to get better all the time.
Got the radio on.
They just played 'Remember me, I'm the one who loves you.'
It set my old ticker to pounding.

Charlie's love letter

Molly was becoming highly suspicious, almost to the point of paranoia, that their co-workers - and perhaps even Muriel, George and her beloved father, Jesse – knew what was going on between herself and Charlie. They agreed to stop holding the card games as two couples, in case it was simply parading their feelings for each other in front of George and Muriel.

Molly wondered if she was a home-wrecker, and hated herself for even the notion of it. Often, when she closed her eyes she could picture a pregnant Muriel and her three beautiful children, all crying their eyes out, or the image of her stern-faced father scolding her for her terrible sin.

But was it really a sin to love someone? Because she did love Charlie, she knew that now, and with a certainty and a fervor that she had never known before. Tommy had been a husband on paper only, and while George had been loving and generous in so many ways, and she did love him in the manner of a sweet, gentle companion, it was true that in recent years she had felt increasingly like one of George's possessions, as if she were a new motorbike, or a cruise through the Baltics.

Charlie always did his best to console her when these fears began to take over, assuring her that what they were doing was so right that surely God would take care of the details, and everything would work out the best for all concerned. 'You can't shake my faith on this, Molly,' he told her frequently. 'I know He wouldn't let us feel this way if He didn't have a plan for us to be together.'

'I don't know that I can ever agree with that, Charlie,' she responded. 'We both took marriage vows.'

'I know,' he said, his eyes reflecting a concern that he didn't always express. 'And I meant every word of them. I just feel,' he continued, grasping her hand, 'that I said those words to the wrong person.'

And she knew what he meant. She had gone through two wedding ceremonies, and was committed to every word she uttered in each of them, but it didn't stop her realising that sometimes, life changed.

It changed even more when they went to the cabin at the lake.

For some time now, their kissing had been becoming more intense. Molly could feel stirrings in her body that had never been so strong, and she knew that Charlie was feeling the same way. It was if she hadn't minded George's impotency until Charlie had awakened her sexuality.

The chance to spend a whole night together was becoming an increasingly sweet prospect. Molly could hardly begin to imagine the joy of being held, caressed, intimate with the man who loved her more than life itself, as he revealed to her constantly through his impassioned love letters. He even called himself 'her husband' in the notes, and she had begun to respond in kind and even allow herself to dream of a time when that might become a reality.

It was Molly herself who opened the way to a few hours in each other's arms becoming a possibility.

'Now George is Vice President, he's always away,' she commented idly to Charlie one day, thinking they might be able to enjoy some time at the movies again.

'He leaves you on your own?' Charlie shook his head, as if that was impossible to believe.

Molly laughed. 'For days at a time.'

She felt the air crackle between them.

'So what do you do,' asked Charlie casually, 'when George is out of town?'

'I usually stay at my father's, or sometimes at a girlfriend's.' Molly held her breath, hardly able to believe what she was about to say. 'He's away for three days early next week.'

Charlie's bold expression took her breath away, and he held her hand for a moment. 'Leave it with me, my darling girl,' he said, and Molly forced herself to hold on. Hold on to that hope, and his love.

He found a cabin, somehow. It belonged to Danny's uncle, and rested by a lake not too far away where his uncle and others would go for fishing outings.

'We could fish all day, and be together all night,' whispered Charlie. 'My two favorite pastimes!'

'I'm not sure I like being put on the same footing as a trout,' Molly told him.

Charlie laughed, and cupped her face in his hands. 'You are not on the same footing as anything or anyone on this earth,' he said earnestly. 'Just a pedestal, up with the angels.'

'You're a smooth talker for a tools and supplies man.' But she kissed him, nonetheless. 'Just a few hours, to begin with.'

Charlie nodded. A few hours would be Heaven. Heaven by the lake.

On Tuesday after work, Molly parked her car about a block away and waited for Charlie, and they drove to the cabin, silent with anticipation. Charlie held the door open for her and then kissed her as the door swung closed behind them. Then he led her to the bedroom, and they walked directly to the bed.

'We should get undressed,' said Charlie, tugging Molly's blouse free from her skirt.

'No.' She felt unaccountably shy, more nervous than she had been with either of her husbands. 'Let's just lie here. I don't want to move too fast.'

They were both shaking with excitement as they laid down, side by side, and began to exchange eager kisses while gently caressing each other. The kissing grew more intense, and Molly felt heat rising up her torso, her neck, her lips feeling scorched with passion. Charlie's hand lighted on her stockings and began to push her skirt up toward her waist, but she gripped his wrist urgently.

'Not any higher, please,' she whispered.

Charlie groaned, but immediately lowered his hand down her legs, stroking the tender insides of her thighs until she felt she might explode. She writhed beneath him, feeling his desire escalating and taking a hold of him in a way that George had never been able to show. She held herself apart from him as long as she could, wishing that she were no longer married, that she could permit her lover to become one with her. His hands rose to her blouse, reaching beneath it to fondle her breasts through the delicate silk of her brassiere. He moved to push it upwards but again she stilled his hand.

'I can't, Charlie,' she told him.

'It's fine,' he returned. 'Whatever you want to do or not do, that's fine. I'm just so happy to be here with you.'

And they continued this way for nearly two hours before they reluctantly broke away. This time, they'd agreed, Molly would go home to Jesse's and get a good night's sleep before going to work in the morning. She doubted, somehow, that she would ever have a good night's sleep again.

For the entire day after their tryst Charlie peppered her with love notes and letters, all expressing awe and joy at what had happened the night before. Molly felt herself blushing more with each note, and eventually had to visit the stock room.

'You have to stop,' she hissed to Charlie. 'I must look as guilty as anything.'

Charlie closed his eyes, remembering. 'No. I know exactly what you look like.'

'Charlie, please stop. Your notes are turning me tomato red. We're still married, and I don't want to cause any gossip.'

At last, Charlie nodded. 'All right,' he said, 'but only if you agree to meet me again tomorrow night.'

And she knew that nothing on earth could stop her.

Now that she knew where she was going, Molly drove herself to the cabin and let herself in, walking around dreamily as if this was her home, and she was just waiting for her husband to arrive.

Then he did arrive, and they walked to the bedroom like newly-weds, holding hands, locking onto each other's eyes. It was difficult to remind herself that they were both close to forty years old, and married to other people.

They caressed each other, moving together as if they were one. Molly had never experienced anything like it, and this time when Charlie's hands reached for the clasp of her brassiere, she didn't stop him, relishing instead the heat of his lips on the delicate skin as he kissed and fondled her breasts.

'Molly,' he moaned, 'I can hardly hold back. They're the most beautiful breasts I've ever seen, ever imagined.'

His words ignited her passion still further, until she simply had to push him away.

'I can't, Charlie,' she gasped. 'Not while we're married. Not like this.'

Charlie's head sank to her shoulder.

'I know,' he said. 'I understand. You know I would never have dreamed of stepping out on Muriel. I just can't seem to help myself.'

She understood that exactly. It was precisely how she felt herself.

Charlie stood abruptly and pulled on his trousers. 'Okay,' he said resolutely. 'Then that's decided. Come on, Molly, get dressed.'

'Where are we going?'

Charlie's actions had surprised her. One moment he'd been lying in her embrace, the next he was almost out the door.

'You're going to your father's,' he said, kissing the back of her hand.

'And what about you?'

Charlie gave her the longest, slowest smile, that didn't quite tally with the sadness in his eyes.

'I'm going to ask Muriel for a divorce.'

Molly drove home in a daze. How had it come to this so quickly? True, their love had been growing for months now – Muriel was about to have her fourth baby in a week or so, for crying out loud – but suddenly she was confronted with how far they had come. It had reached a point of no return, she knew. They couldn't carry on like this. Neither of them had intended it, and neither of them wanted to be disloyal to their spouses. But if their meetings at the cabin had told her anything, it was that neither of them had ever known love like this. It was deep and devout, and they owed it to all concerned to make a go of it, properly and decently.

So, after a restless night in her old bed back at Jesse's, Molly called in sick to the factory, and went home to wait for George.

He looked surprised to find her there as he came through the door, but then he saw her slumped demeanor. Instantly, he put his bag down and rushed to her side.

'You've been crying,' he said, holding her hand. 'Is it Jesse?'

The last time he'd seen her this upset was when Aunt Dolores died, so it was a typically reasonable question from her attentive and reasonable husband.

Molly shook her head slowly. 'Dad's fine, George. It's … it's us.'

'Us?'

'We need to part.'

'You mean – divorce?' George stood up quickly, moving to the fireplace where he could see Molly's face.

He didn't sound terribly surprised.

Molly nodded. 'I do love you, George, but I …'

'There's someone else,' he finished for her.

She nodded again, her face ablaze with shame.

Then he shocked her still more. 'It's Charlie, I assume?' When she didn't answer immediately, he went on: 'You should give it some serious thought before taking such drastic action. Charlie's a family man with three, nearly four children to support. I'm not sure Muriel will let him go all that easily.' He crossed to Molly's side and picked up her limp hand. 'And we have a comfortable life, Molly. An exciting, comfortable life. You should think twice before giving that up, too.'

'I know, George. Every word of that is true,' said Molly, fighting to hold back tears. 'And I wasn't looking for anything else, I promise you. But with Charlie, everything is different.'

George let out a bitter laugh.

'Oh, I'm sure everything's very different. And I can't say I'm entirely shocked. I always thought there was the possibility that you might ask me for a divorce because of ... my sexual difficulties.'

'George, that isn't it at all!' cried Molly. 'I have always loved and respected you, been true to you. I'd never dreamed of asking for a divorce until meeting ... him. And I've been true to my vows, George. I've no intention of having relations until after I'm divorced.'

'You haven't already?' snapped George.

'No, we haven't.'

George's face paled to a sickly grey. 'Does everyone know? The people at the factory, are they remembering the silly old confirmed bachelor who married the beautiful girl from work? Does Muriel know?'

'Muriel may know by now.' Molly slipped an arm around her husband's waist. 'But nobody's laughing at you, George. Least of all me. You have given me a beautiful life, and I know that it's my own fault if I haven't appreciated that enough. I would never allow anyone to laugh at you.'

George nodded slowly, passing a hand over his creased features.

'I know that. And I understand, Molly. I just need ... I need some time to think about it.'

'I never meant to hurt you,' said Molly, starting to cry again. 'It's the last thing I wanted.'

'Don't cry, old girl.' George patted her shoulder in a familiar, comforting manner. 'We'll work things out.'

And Molly truly hoped, for all their sakes, that they really could.

Chapter 16

And Baby Makes Six

Pillow talk, pillow talk;
Another night of bein' alone with pillow talk
When it's all said and done,
Two heads together can be better than one

Doris Day, *Pillow Talk*

Charlie arrived home to find his mother-in-law pacing anxiously on the front porch. His heart plummeted as soon as he saw her, very evidently waiting for him.

He'd told Muriel that he was meeting Danny to go bowling; maybe she'd checked with Danny, somehow, and his friend hadn't managed to cover for him convincingly enough. Given what he was planning to do, it seemed odd to hope that Muriel hadn't found out about him and Molly, but he had wanted her to hear it from him. Directly. In the strange circumstances in which they'd found themselves, it seemed like the decent way to proceed.

'Where have you been?' cried Betty as he flung open the car door. 'Muriel's been asking for you for an hour!'

'Why?' said Charlie, not answering her question. 'Is everything okay?'

Betty grabbed him by the arm to propel him through the door more quickly. 'She's in labor, poor child.'

The baby wasn't due for another ten days. Charlie ran to the bedroom from where he could hear strenuous screaming and some choice curses that the other children did not need to know.

'Muriel, I'm here.' Charlie ran to Muriel's side of their bed and reached for her hand. She gripped it as if she wanted to crush his bones. 'How are you doing?'

'I'm having the baby too soon!' she screamed. 'How do you think I'm doing?'

'Okay, okay.' He turned to Betty who was hovering in the doorway with Detty and one of the twins. Where the other one had crawled to, he had no idea. 'Betty, do you think she needs to go to the hospital? I know most births take place at home once you've had as many children as Muriel, but what with the complications with the twins …'

'Take me to the hospital!' roared Muriel before Betty even had time to reply. 'This second!'

'Right.' Charlie hauled Muriel into a roughly-seated position and scooped her up into his arms. 'The car's right outside.'

'I'll take care of the little ones,' said Betty, herding the children away from the bedroom door. 'You just look after Muriel and the baby.'

'I will,' promised Charlie, his heart pounding when he thought about what he'd just been about to do. How could he ask his wife for a divorce when she was giving birth to his fourth child?

'Faster, Charlie! I want to get there faster!'

Muriel was practically hysterical now. He laid her out as well as he could across the back seat of the car, remembering, just for a moment, the last time he'd been told to go as fast as he could. He'd been a child, really, though he was only a few years younger than Muriel was now. And here he sat, behind the wheel of a roadster, about to speed away to save the life of his own child.

In that moment, Charlie realized that he would do anything, always, for the lives of his children, and if that meant giving up Molly and staying with Muriel forever, then that was how it would have to be. His chest ached with the prospect of it, but he ignored the sensation as he raced into the town to the hospital, with Muriel shrieking from the back seat so that he feared he might have to stop the car and deliver the baby himself.

Thankfully they made it to the hospital before their fourth child presented himself to the world. Running into the reception area, Charlie looked around for anyone medical, and seized the white coat of a passing doctor.

'My wife,' he panted, 'she's having a baby. It's ten days early.'

The doctor, in his late twenties and looking impossibly young to be a qualified medical adviser, spun around immediately, snapping orders at the staff. 'Where is she, sir?'

'In the car. Back seat.'

'You and you,' barked the doctor to a couple of orderlies with an authority that belied his years, 'help the lady out of the car, and stretcher her if needs be. Nurse Hatton, prepare the surgeon in case there's an emergency operation needed.

Sir,' he said to Charlie, 'don't be worried. Your wife is in the best hands now. What's her name?'

Charlie sank onto a chair. 'Muriel,' he said, exhausted, despondent and exhilarated at the same time. Not Molly. Maybe he'd never get to say Molly. 'My wife's name is Muriel.'

The doctor hesitated for a moment, frowning at Charlie. Then he excused himself and ran outside to help the orderlies bring Muriel inside. He was patting her hand reassuringly as Muriel's prone body shot past Charlie, her face scarlet from screaming.

'The baby's coming soon,' said Nurse Hatton to Charlie. 'You can go and wait in the room near the maternity ward, and we'll let you know when Baby is here.'

'Thank you,' said Charlie.

He made his way to the room where the fathers congregated, glad to see that only one other father-to-be was in there, chain-smoking and marching in zig-zags up and down the tiled floor. The man offered Charlie a cigarette.

'Thank you, but I don't smoke,' he responded.

'First?' asked the other father.

Charlie shook his head. 'Fourth.'

'Four?' The man laughed. 'You'll be used to all this, then. It's my first. I'm terrified.'

'It'll be fine,' said Charlie.

'So they keep telling me,' the other replied, before resuming his frantic marching.

Charlie leaned against the window, thinking about what he'd said. "It'll be fine." He'd been promised that himself, decades ago, before the bank robbery. He'd promised his wife that everything would be fine, and yet she'd had difficulties giving birth to the twins, and now a baby on the way too early, and she wasn't even aware of what bad news Charlie had just been about to impart.

And Molly. He'd promised her so often that it would be fine, that it would work out, that God must have meant for them to be together to have filled each of them with so much love for the other, and yet he couldn't swear to her now that everything would work out as they'd hoped. It will be fine. Had there ever been four words that were more ill-used? He couldn't think of any, just the three special words that he'd repeated to Molly over and over, from the very bottom of his heart.

Nurse Hatton tapped on the glass, beaming, and gestured to the other man to come outside. His baby had arrived. 'Guess I'm a father!' he said deliriously.

Charlie nodded, and shook his hand.

'How's my wife doing?' he asked the nurse.

'I'll go and see,' she said, 'just as soon as I've taken Mr Green to see his new baby.'

'Of course.'

Charlie's mind began to wander. What if Muriel's health was compromised? She might die! What would he do then, with a cluster of tiny children? Would Molly want anything to do with him then? Or could he just learn to love Muriel properly, the way he loved Molly?

'It'll be fine,' he told his reflection, although somehow he doubted it.

Suddenly his thoughts were interrupted by the arrival of the doctor who had met him in reception.

'Hello again,' he said in his confident, clipped tone. 'So you're Muriel's husband?'

Charlie was taken aback. What an odd question! 'Yes,' he said. 'Still the same husband that brought her in.'

The doctor stared at him and then gave a curt nod. 'She's doing fine. The baby was breech but we've managed to turn it around, so she's giving birth naturally. It might be another half hour or so.'

'Oh, thank the Lord,' said Charlie, feeling his knees give way. 'Take care of them both, doc.'

'It will be my pleasure,' replied the doctor.

He gave Charlie another once over, then closed the door behind him, leaving Charlie with the feeling that he hadn't quite measured up to some standard or other.

The doctor was true to his word, though. Less than an hour later, Nurse Hatton returned to the waiting room. 'Your turn now,' she said with a broad smile.

She led him along the corridor to a glass-fronted room, and pointed to the second child along. Charlie could only see a small, perfectly round head, and the wriggling of some tiny feet.

'Seven and a half pounds,' the nurse told him. 'That's big for a breech birth. Your young wife managed valiantly.'

'She always does,' said Charlie, hating himself at that moment.

Then she directed him to the maternity ward where Doctor Manson was waiting beside Muriel's bed. She gave Charlie a wan smile and waved the doctor away.

'Another girl,' she said weakly. 'Wanted to fight her way out of there.'

Charlie kissed her forehead and sat down beside her. 'Our children are all fighters.'

Even now, he was very aware of the young doctor hovering a few beds away.

'Are you all right?' Charlie nodded toward Manson. 'He seems worried about you.'

'I'm fine,' said Muriel, 'for someone who just had another complicated birth.'

'Good, I'm glad—' Charlie started to say, but Muriel hadn't finished.

'And for someone whose husband was missing when she went into labor.'

The room seemed to turn cold. Muriel was gazing at him from the pillow, and from behind, he could feel Manson's eyes boring into his back.

'Muriel, I was … I didn't know the baby was coming. I'd have come straight home if I'd realised.' He took hold of her hand. 'I'm sorry.'

He wouldn't tell her. He couldn't tell her now. It would be too hurtful.

But suddenly Muriel laughed. 'You were with her, weren't you? Molly.' She watched Charlie's face as it shifted from shock to guilt, and then laughed again. 'It's fine. I like Molly very much. I've always suspected you might leave me for her, ever since we played cards with her and George.'

Charlie shook his head. 'I don't know what to say.'

'How about, "Muriel, should we get a divorce?"'

She sounded incredibly calm about it all. Charlie could hardly believe what he was hearing. 'A divorce?'

Muriel shrugged. 'We both know this hasn't worked out the way we both dreamed. There's seventeen years between us, for a start. We have babies in common, but not a lot else. You're still a sweet man, though, Charlie. You deserve to be happy.'

She squeezed his hand as he marveled at her levelheadedness. 'But what will you do? I mean, obviously, I'll provide for the children and see them on a regular basis, until they're eighteen years old and ready to head out into the world on their own two feet.'

'That's eighteen years exactly for our latest wee daughter,' said Muriel. 'Are you sure you can keep that pledge?'

Charlie laid his hand across his heart. 'I promise to always look out for our babies, in every way possible. And you, Muriel. I'll take care of you financially, even if you marry again. It's the least I can do.'

'Even if?' Muriel laughed. 'I might even be re-married before you, Charlie.'

'There's ... you've met someone else?'

Muriel simply smiled mysteriously, but suddenly the strange comments and glances from Doctor Manson – who'd obviously met Muriel on at least four occasions – made a lot more sense.

'We'll just say we're incompatible as I'm so young and lively and you're ... you,' said Muriel cheekily. 'And that way, we can get divorced as soon as possible.'

Charlie kissed her cheek, and for the longest time they held hands as Doctor Manson hopped around near the end of the ward. 'I married well, Muriel,' said Charlie eventually.

'Me too,' she replied. 'Now, go and fetch our baby.'

Charlie stood in a daze, stopping in front of Doctor Manson for a moment to shake his hand, and then heading out of the ward in search of his new daughter.

As he reached the door, Muriel called his name.

'It'll be fine, Charlie,' she said, nodding. 'You'll see.'

And this time, he believed those words completely.

Chapter 17

Two Couples Parting

She just happened to feel like it. Wasn't that after all, the only reason there was? Had she ever had a less selfish, more complicated reason for doing anything in her life?"

Revolutionary Road, Richard Yates

When Molly heard, as she returned to work having confronted George, that Charlie was at home because Muriel had just given birth to their fourth baby, her heart leapt into her throat. How could she expect Charlie to mention divorce to his wife at this juncture?

And now it might be too late for her. She had already come clean to George. He hadn't spoken to her since - just packed his briefcase and headed off to his factory without comment, calling to say that he was staying in a hotel that night while he mulled things over.

Molly didn't have Charlie's issues when it came to a divorce. She wasn't Catholic, for a start. She and George didn't have children. On paper, it would seem that Molly's separation from George should prove to be much more straightforward.

But now there were four children involved, and the ever-increasing chance that George might just refuse to cooperate.

When Charlie didn't show up for work for a second day, Molly made the excuse of being ill – she certainly felt sick - and went home. She planned at first to drive past Charlie's house, but then realised that, with four children under four years old, there was a high likelihood of someone being out front playing with one of them.

She headed home with a knot in her stomach that underlined what an idiot she'd been. How could she have been so foolish as to act in haste, with no guarantees for the future? She felt every bit as adrift in life as she had when her mother had died, all those years ago.

The twisted stomach worsened when she saw George's car in the driveway. It was unusual for him to be home earlier than six pm, but then, these were unusual times. She put her key in the lock carefully, half-expecting the locks to be changed, but it clicked open as always, and she stepped into the hall.

'You're early,' said her husband from the dining room.

'I wasn't feeling well,' she said, offering him a peck on the cheek.

He accepted it gently, then motioned to the table. The surface was covered in documents, neatly packaged into files with George's steady hand-writing, so different to Charlie's impassioned scrawl in his love notes, topping each pile of papers with a title: House, or Will, and Retirement.

'I've been to see Gerald Lassiter,' he said. 'I'm not one to abandon my wife, even if she is leaving me to be with another man. I want you to be supported in the future.'

'You're agreeing to the divorce?'

George nodded slowly.

'Oh, George. You don't need to do anything else for me.'

'I want to,' he said sincerely. 'We've spent nearly ten years being happily married, and you faithfully gave me your unconditional love. We never had a cross word between us, and you must admit that we've enjoyed each other's company.'

'Of course.'

'It's been a wonderful adventure, Molly.' George spoke sadly but with a determination she hadn't heard the night she'd broached the idea of divorce. 'This last decade has been the best period of my life, by far, spoiled only by my impotence. But even that hasn't been an issue. You never complained, or made me feel embarrassed or inadequate. Quite the contrary, in fact. You've been a wonderful wife to me, and I will always love and respect you.'

'And I you,' whispered Molly, close to tears.

George sighed, then straightened his back. 'I can see that Charlie really loves you, and I want you to be happy. Of course, he is leaving a wife and three children.'

'Four, now,' said Molly. George's eyes widened. 'But he'll always support them – I'll make sure of it.' She wasn't sure she'd be with him while he did it, or even if he could leave Muriel now, but that was something for a later discussion.

'He's ... he's a decent man,' said George. 'I always liked him. And I hope in time that we can all remain friends.'

Molly was, quite simply, stunned. She went to embrace George again, and he allowed himself a brief moment in her arms as she told him that she didn't deserve him, before angling her into a chair and passing her a cup of coffee.

He then proceeded to give Molly a rundown on what he and Lassiter had drawn up, for Molly to receive after the divorce decree. Firstly, his attorney would file for a non-contested divorce based on incompatibility due to their age difference. Next, George would give Molly an amount of money matching that in her independent savings account. That would mean her savings account would end up amounting to four times her present annual salary.

'Thirdly,' he said, passing her a copy of another set of papers, 'on the first business day after the granting of the divorce, an account will be set up in your name containing enough money to buy a house for yourself – and Charlie. He'll need to divert his own earnings to Muriel and the children, and I won't have my ex-wife living in anything less than the manner to which she's become accustomed.'

'George, it's too much,' Molly protested, but George held up a hand.

'I didn't want this,' he said gently, 'but if it has to happen, I want it to be civilized and straightforward. I want to make sure there's every opportunity for us to remain close afterwards. So much so that I've asked Gerald if he'll handle Charlie and Muriel's divorce if they want that. I'll pay the costs.'

With the same sad smile that had ghosted his features for days, George handed Molly a folder to put her copies in. She took it, and then sat down on George's lap, giving him a loving hug and kiss. 'I'm so grateful, George. For everything.'

He pushed her away before too long. 'And how is Charlie's divorce progressing?' he ventured, as civil as any divorcing Vice President could be.

Molly didn't have the heart to tell him that she had no idea, not of how it was going, or even if it was going ahead.

'Don't torture yourself,' she told George instead.

If anyone should be torturing themselves, it was her.

One way to do it would be visiting her father, and letting him know what had gone on. She steeled herself for the uproar, and began to drive slowly toward her father's house.

But suddenly there he was, on the sidewalk near her home, obviously building himself up to knock on her door.

The car slowed to a halt beside him.

'Charlie,' she cried.

He flung open the door and dragged her to him. 'You weren't at work! I went in to tell you what happened, and you weren't there.'

'Muriel had the baby,' she said as he rained kisses on her face and neck.

'Yes, and she agreed to a divorce.' Charlie stood back to watch her face as the news sank in. 'Amazing, isn't it? I think she's been seeing someone else – a doctor. She wanted it more than me. Faster than me.'

'Oh, Charlie, that's staggering.'

'So we … will you be brave, my darling, and talk to George?'

Molly laughed. 'I already have! I didn't know that you'd done it though. I've been so frightened. I was just driving to my father's to throw myself on his mercy.'

'And … did George agree?'

Molly nodded, and Charlie yanked her straight out of the car, yelling and spinning her around on the sidewalk until she was dizzy with joy.

Then she sat him down in the passenger seat of her car and told him how much George had just agreed to do for her. For them.

Charlie looked close to crying. 'I've known some good men in my life, Molly. Mr Adams, my attorney. Warden Kelly. All the priests who've guided me. But George is a saint. God really has been guiding us, and I know he'll continue to watch over us for the rest of our lives together. Our marriage,' he said, grasping her hand, 'will be made in heaven.'

'And what about Muriel and the children?'

Charlie tapped the dashboard thoughtfully, then smiled at Molly. 'I have an idea, if you're agreeable …'

Charlie's divorce proceedings had hit a snag, so he and Muriel had lined up an appointment with their attorney that Saturday morning. The lawyer had contacted Muriel, telling her that the judge would require signed papers from Charlie, guaranteeing a reasonable level of support from him for Muriel and the children. She'd explained that she was happy with the arrangement, but the attorney had insisted.

Armed with his new information, Charlie and Muriel marched into the attorney's office on the Saturday morning, and Charlie took the floor, almost as he remembered Mr Adams doing all those years ago.

'I don't know who you think you are, Mr Cranhorn, to be meddling with these arrangements.' Charlie slapped the envelope in his hand with the back of the other. 'Muriel gave you specific instructions about our divorce which you have failed to follow. You have no business taking it on your own head to proceed without getting permission from us.'

Cranhorn rocked back in his chair. 'Now, see here, it's my responsibility to determine how the judge might rule on the case, and make sure it's strong enough to ensure it will be approved. I concur that I should have obtained your permission before instructing your wife as I did, but I did so with good reason.'

'So how did you determine what the court will require from me?'

'Based on my experiences in previous cases.' The attorney was flushed, but still looking self-assured.

Muriel then spoke up. 'We wanted this sorted quickly. You've had this for over two weeks, and there's still no sign of it being filed any time soon.'

'That's right,' said Charlie, suddenly thinking of something. 'And I bet for every day that passes, you're charging us more.'

The attorney turned an even deeper shade of crimson. 'You don't understand what this work entails …' he started feebly.

Charlie squared up to his desk. 'I understand this. As a couple, we have agreed to this divorce. And as a couple, we have agreed that I am in the lucky position of being able to devote almost my entire income to the support of Muriel and the children.'

'Nearly all of it!' agreed Muriel triumphantly.

'Do you think that would be enough for the judge?'

Mr Cranhorn shifted uncomfortably in his seat. 'I did not know that.'

'No,' said Charlie scathingly. 'You just assumed. But you never can tell how much people know, Mr Cranhorn.'

Charlie offered Muriel his arm, and she held onto him regally. 'Goodbye, Mr Cranhorn,' she said with beguiling sweetness. 'And by the way, you're fired.'

'I think we'll go to Mr Lassiter, shall we, Muriel?'

'Indeed we shall, Charlie.'

Mr Cranhorn glared at them from behind his owl glasses. 'You'll be receiving my bill in the mail,' he called after them.

But Charlie and his soon-to-be former wife were already way down the corridor. On his way to a divorce, thought Charlie. That was supposed to be a terrible thing for a good Catholic like himself, but somehow, the whole thing seemed to be almost satisfying. He gave Muriel a hug as she expressed her own delight at what had just transpired, and headed for the car.

He felt like a drive.

The open road.

Top speed.

Chapter 18

A Marriage Made in Heaven

And I'm convinced the angels must have sent you
And they meant you just for me

Don Lockwood in Singing in the Rain

The day after Molly's divorce from George was finalized, the lovers eloped to an adjacent state where there was no waiting period to obtain a marriage license, to be married right away by a Justice of the Peace.

They had taken a week of vacation, but not made any particular plans for a honeymoon. Then Danny suggested the cabin on the lake. It was available for a week, if they wanted to use it.

'It's a wonderful idea,' Molly had said. 'We can have a whole week together in solitude. Just focusing on our love for each other, without interruptions.'

'And it does have special memories for us,' said Charlie. 'Not to mention a huge amount of fishing gear.'

Molly pulled a face. 'Well, I don't know about that. I was thinking more about romantic excursions around the lake in the boat.'

'Whatever my love desires,' Charlie had said, hardly daring to believe that, after all their devotion and trials, he would take Molly there as his wife.

After the service and a celebratory lunch at an old, historically famous hotel, they drove toward the cabin. On the way there, Molly discovered that her husband had a 'lead foot'. About halfway to the lake, they were stopped for speeding by a friendly highway patrolman, who found out they were on honeymoon and issued them with a warning notice rather than a ticket. He sent them on their way after shaking Charlie's hand.

Now, finally, they arrived at the cabin. Their haven.

They made their way to the bedroom and held each other close in the doorway before the freedom of their marriage and their new situation finally hit them. They began to disrobe, shedding all their clothing and underwear. Charlie held Molly in his arms, allowing his hands to roam over the length of her willowy body, before laying her gently on the bed. He stroked her thighs as he had before, and this time strayed higher and higher, to the delight of his new wife, before Charlie realized the dream he had held so vividly in his mind for so long, since a few weeks after first meeting Molly.

Making love with his dream lady was even more heavenly than he had thought it would be. As he rose to a climax, Molly was moaning with delight, which greatly added to Charlie's pleasure. She was trembling with such passion that Charlie had an impulse to melt into her body, to become one with her, and suddenly she cried out and he knew that all his dreams had come true in one beautiful, united moment.

Afterwards they lay side-by-side, whispering of their love for each other as Charlie traced the shapes on Molly's beautiful face. Ten minutes or so later, Charlie was ready to make love again. Molly seemed surprised, but she cooperated eagerly, her evident satisfaction even more intense than it had been the first time, and when Charlie made love to her a third time, lasting much longer than previously, Molly was beside herself, crying out in ecstasy.

For Charlie, too, it was a sexual pleasure way beyond anything he had ever experienced with Muriel, and he realised that their chemistry was yet another indicator of their abiding love. They were both on cloud nine, both absolutely convinced – if there was any lingering doubt – that they were truly made for each other. This was how they would spend the rest of their lives together, joined by passion and understanding and the deepest of love – if two vessels alone could contain such love ...

The afternoon, the evening, the night passed in a dream. In the morning, they had made love, and now they were lying side-by-side, exhausted but content. The morning sun was streaming through the window, shining on their glistening bodies as Charlie rolled over and stood up. Molly continued to lie there, relaxed and smiling like an angel, as a shaft of sunlight beamed through the window, anointing her body with light like the angel he had told her she was. Charlie stood there, transfixed. What a beautiful body. How lucky he was to have Molly love him. To call her his wife. Abandoning his plans to get up, Charlie climbed back into bed beside her ...

They breakfasted simply on some provisions they'd brought, but by late afternoon they were hungry. They stopped at a filling station for gas, and the attendant suggested they consider a very popular restaurant, The Amish House, which was about five miles out of town.

As they approached, they noticed how full the parking lot was, and that many cars were parked on both sides up and down the road. They pulled in and managed to find a spot, then entered the restaurant to the buzz of conversation and laughter as crowds of people milled around.

An Amish receptionist greeted them, and on finding out that they were first time customers, informed them they had the option of going through the food line or ordering from their table. They chose the line, discovering a wide selection of meats, vegetables, breads, condiments and deserts – all typical homemade Amish fare.

Molly selected a slice of prime rib, mashed potatoes and gravy, green beans, biscuits, bread pudding, and a glass of apple cider. Charlie selected two slices of ham, baked sweet potatoes, green beans, cornbread, custard pudding, and a glass of apple cider. As they were enjoying their delicious dinner at their table, a young, pretty waitress brought them a glass of water, and informed them that they could go through the line as often as they wanted to - or she or one of the other waitresses could bring them anything they wanted to order. The price was the same, no matter how many dishes, or how much, they ate.

In talking to the waitress, they found out that the employees, all dressed in typical Amish attire, were mostly from the two families who operated the restaurant, and the rest of them were aunts, uncles and cousins. All the dishes were prepared by the extended family members. It was truly a family affair, with every one of the dishes home cooked. As the waitress brought them another glass of cider, Charlie excused himself to go through the line again to get another piece of cornbread, a dish of navy beans and ham, and a dish of bread pudding.

When they left their table to go to the cashier to pay their bill, they discovered that there was another wing of the building containing a bakery, a candy shop, and four rooms filled with knick-knacks, handicrafts, linens, and furniture - all home-made and hand-crafted by members of the Amish community. From that day on, The Amish House became their favorite restaurant and place to shop, where they always dined when they ate out when staying at the lake, and even frequently drove to from their home to dine there on weekends.

The six days they spent at the cabin were a truly classical romantic idyll. The balmy, bright, sunny days were spent strolling, hand-in-hand, on the wooded paths along the lake shore. They rowed the boat around the lake, anchoring in spots that appeared to contain a lot of large, hungry, fish, just waiting to be caught, fishing at those spots for an hour or two to land an incredible number of keeper-sized fish - mainly Large-Mouth Bass, Channel Catfish, and fat Blue Gill.

The days were punctuated, of course, by romantic interludes in the cabin, Molly showing her pleasure as much as Charlie and admitting to him that, after eighteen years of marriage, first to Tommy and then to George, this was the first time she had ever known sexual satisfaction. Love she had experienced, but this was something new.

They ate all three meals, each day, at The Amish House. An unexpected bonus in going regularly to the Restaurant, and getting to know many of the Amish people who worked there, was that they appreciatively accepted all the fish that Charlie and Molly caught. Molly actually caught more fish than Charlie, and despite her initial reluctance, from that time forward she became an avid fisherwoman. On two of the afternoons they were there, a family fish fry was held on the patio behind the restaurant. Charlie and Molly were honored guests, not only for contributing the fish, but also because they were on their honeymoon.

In the balmy evenings, before retiring to nights of exciting love making, interspersed with periods of sound sleeping, they often daubed their skin with mosquito repellent and lounged in comfortable chairs on the boat dock, watching the sun set and the moon rise. Their idyllic honeymoon at the lake was the happiest period in Molly's life. And as for Charlie, he truly believed he'd found Heaven on earth.

Until they could find a place to rent near the factory, Molly had arranged for herself and Charlie to stay with Jesse. Very reluctantly, Jesse had agreed, saying they could stay in her old room for as long as they needed to.

'Why don't you like him, Dad?' she'd asked, although she already knew the answer.

'I don't really know him,' he replied, unwilling to share his evident dislike.

'Is it because he was married before? Because I was too. This is my second divorce.'

Jesse's eyes narrowed. 'That's as may be, Molly, but you didn't go breaking up a family.'

'He's going to look after her properly, and the children,' she assured him. 'We both are.'

'And who else was he married to? What happened to that wife?'

Molly wasn't sure what he meant, but then worked out that he'd calculated that Charlie must have been married before, as he was so much older than Muriel. She took a deep breath. 'He wasn't married before, Dad. He was in prison. For twenty years.'

She told him Charlie's tale of incarceration, and Jesse heaved himself up to make coffee.

'Got yourself a fine one, there, Molly,' he said quietly, and she had bitten back a retort about how much he'd approved of Tommy, and what a "fine one" he turned out to be.

Now they set about moving back into her bedroom, beside Maureen who was also still there, though her sons had moved out with even the youngest at college in Colorado. Maureen was dating a widower with a very nice house of his own, and both she and Jesse were hopeful that she'd move into it if they married. For now, it was nice for Molly to have some support in the frosty atmosphere that surrounded her marriage to Charlie.

They returned to work on Monday, and were instantly confronted by their co-workers about their marriage – and Molly about her divorce from George.

'I can't believe you kept it all so quiet,' bleated Annette from her coveted place at their lunch table. 'And George, how's he? Maybe I should have married him! Oh,' she said, thinking aloud, 'maybe I still can!'

Molly had to laugh. 'Maybe you can,' she said, as Charlie winked and stirred salt into his soup. 'He's a lovely, decent man. I enjoyed being married to George, and we are remaining very good friends.'

'And what about Muriel?' Danny slid into place beside Charlie. 'Who's going to look after her and all those children you kept having?'

'Well, not that it's any of your business,' said Charlie evenly, 'but Muriel is very well looked after – she's even got my new car - and I'll be supporting the kids until they've all graduated from high school.'

'So …' mused Danny, the confirmed bachelor, 'Muriel's single again.'

Charlie laughed. 'I don't think so, but feel free to find out for yourself.'

Within a few weeks, they were working in an atmosphere that was nearly the same as it had been before their wedding, except that now they almost always ate lunch together, and they never again passed secret notes to each other.

Chapter 19

There's No Place Like Home

Now I shout it from the highest hills
Even told the golden daffodils
At last, my life's an open door
And my secret love's no secret any more

Calamity Jane (Doris Day)

They ended up spending nearly two weeks at Jesse's house, before finding a nice rental home within walking distance of their work, during which time both Jesse and Maureen warmed up to Charlie.

The newly-weds had decided that they would both work at their current jobs until they qualified for a pension, which meant approximately seven years for Molly and seventeen for Charlie. They would live on Molly's income, supplemented by withdrawals from her savings as needed, and they would give most of Charlie's pay check to Muriel for support of her and the children. In the case of Muriel getting remarried, they would cut Charlie's contribution for support of the children to about fifty percent. When Jesse learned this, he was very pleased, and even more so when he heard that Charlie had given his car to Muriel and paid for her driving lessons. Finally, when he learned that Charlie was an avid fisherman and that Molly was on her way to becoming one herself, he warmed up to Charlie even more. It was clear that, even though he did not believe in divorce, he was now accepting of Charlie being his son-in-law. Molly decided to withhold the information about her financial gifts from George, until a more appropriate time. She was hesitant mainly because she didn't want Maureen to know about it.

On the second weekend at her father's home, they rented a trailer and borrowed Jesse's truck to pull it, moving the small amount of mostly used furniture they had purchased over the past week or so to their new home. They would have a used bed frame, with new box springs, mattress and bed linens, a used kitchen table with four chairs and a used chest of drawers. They also hauled several pieces which her father gave them as a wedding present: an antique settee, a rocking chair, a chenille bedspread, an assortment of kitchen ware, a toaster, and her mother's silverware. He also gave them several boxes of home canned vegetables and fruit, as well as several boxes of potatoes, turnips, onions, tomatoes and green beans from his garden. They would add to their furnishings over the next few months as they shopped around for things which they needed.

For now, they had enough to set up housekeeping in their first home, which was furnished with a small Frigidaire refrigerator, an Amana kitchen stove, and a Whirlpool ringer-style, washer. In the little weedy plot of grass in the backyard, there were two poles strung with rope which served as a clothes-line. The basement included a coal-fired furnace, an ash can, a coal bin, and a lot of shelving for canned goods.

Over the next month or so, they spent most of their free time shopping for their home. Some of the first things which they purchased were an assortment of yard tools including a push grass mower, a hoe, a rake, a soil-turning fork, clippers, and pruning shears. Charlie intended to maintain a nice yard, and to plant vegetable and flower gardens in the Spring.

By the end of two months they had completed the furnishing of their home, stocked their shelves, pantry, and refrigerator with food, and cleaned and trimmed up their yards. Most days, Molly cooked breakfast and dinner for the two of them, and she would wash the dishes and Charlie would dry them and put them away. They ate their lunch in the factory cafeteria, and usually ate out one night during the week and several times on weekends for breakfast, lunch or dinner.

Every other weekend, Charlie helped Molly with washing and drying their laundry. His job was mainly carrying the basket of wet laundry into the back yard, hanging the pieces on the clothes lines, using wooden clothes pins, taking them down when they were dry and carrying the basket into the house for Molly to iron and put away. On laundry days, for several hours, the back yard bloomed with a wide assortment of drying clothing, flapping in the wind. Charlie loved the sweet smell of the air-dried clothing as he took them down and put them in the basket.

In fact, Charlie loved working with his angel for life, setting up and running their first home. Even though it was a rental home, his most common dream while in prison - having a loving wife, like his mother, and owning a home, filled with his children and with the aromas of baked breads and biscuits - was beginning to come true.

The first weekend of their third month of marriage dawned with great weather, so they decided to make a trip over to the lake to see if there were any cabins for sale and to have a meal or two at The Amish House. They had decided that they would probably spend a year or so in their rental home, while they took their time in looking around for a home to buy. In the meantime, they decided, perhaps, to buy a cabin on the lake, where they could go on weekend fishing trips - if they could find one on sale at a reasonable price.

They left for the lake early Saturday morning and arrived at The Amish House in time for an early lunch. Their many Amish friends were happy to see them, and during a delicious and filling lunch, they talked to a few of them about their desire to find an affordable cabin on the lake which they could buy. There were several for sale, and their friends also gave them a note of introduction to a realtor friend of theirs. He confirmed that there were, indeed, at least two properties for sale and that there might be a third that would soon go onto the market. They, then, accepted his invitation to take them to see the two properties that, for sure, were for sale.

They liked both listed properties and were trying to decide between then when the realtor suggested that they stop by to see the third property. They agreed, but when they arrived at the address, they found no indication that it was for sale. However, they noticed a man trimming the shrubbery on the next-door property.

'Hello,' called Charlie. 'Are we right in thinking this place is for sale?'

'I believe so,' said the neighbor, 'although it's not on the market yet.'

'Do you think they'd mind if we looked around?'

Molly could see the potential of it even from the car. The one-acre property had a nice, open stand of large maple, beech, walnut, oak, pines and assorted other trees. It also boasted a nicer dock than the other two properties, with a beautiful motorboat tied up to it.

'Help yourself.'

They examined the exteriors as they walked around the property, and could see some of the interiors by peering through the windows. It was, by far, the nicer of the three properties. The realtor gave the next door neighbor his card. 'Get them to give me a call if they're interested in selling.'

They didn't have long to wait in hearing from the realtor. The owners of the third property would soon be moving to another state, and were willing to sell at a good price if the buyers could pay them immediately in cash – and for that they would throw in the cabin furnishings, nearly everything in the storage sheds, and the motorboat.

'All you'd have to do after buying it would be to move in and immediately enjoy yourselves,' the realtor told them.

In less than an hour Charlie called the realtor back to tell him that they would accept the offer. They would bring a bank cashier's check with them on Saturday, and would hand over the check to the sellers on the spot. In the meantime, the realtor should draw up the papers.

'And I'll bring a check for your fee, too,' said Charlie. 'Half price, I'm assuming, given that it wasn't listed.'

The realtor laughed. 'All right,' he said. 'It was about the easiest sale I've ever done.'

Molly and Charlie looked at each other. There was a sense of ease to it – a feeling that they'd been presented with this house in the same way they'd been given each other. It was meant to be.

They were so excited that they could hardly wait until Saturday.

The realtor drove the three of them to the property, where they were invited into the cabin where they were relieved and not surprised to find that that the interior was beautiful. The five of them spent an hour enjoying coffee and cinnamon rolls, while the previous owners shared information about the property and boat. The boat was only six-years old, and was powered by a 20-horsepower Evenrude engine. It had attachments to make it both more comfortable and more effective for fishing. There were also water skis, in excellent condition, in the storage shed.

On the way back to the realty office, they invited the realtor to join them for lunch at the Amish restaurant. As ever, the food was plentiful. The warm, aromatic biscuits were so good, and so reminiscent of his mother's, that Charlie had Sarah bring him several orders of them, two at a time, lavishing them with butter before experiencing the joy of eating them. Then Charlie and Molly said their goodbyes and drove to their new, beautiful cabin on the lake.

They spent the rest of the day becoming acquainted with their cabin, the contents of the two storage sheds, and the boat and boat dock. The cabin had two bedrooms, one with a queen-size bed and one with a twin-size bed, and a small bathroom, containing a stall shower, a toilet, and a sink, in between. The third room, which took up half of the cabin, served as a living room, dining room, and kitchen combined. The room contained a small oak dining table with four matching chairs; two padded rocking chairs, and a small, leather, three-seat sofa. Each bedroom had a window, the bathroom had a skylight, and the great room had a large picture window, with a view of the lake, above the kitchen sink, and a large window, with a wooded view, on the other side of the room. The interior of the house was very light, which complemented the freshly painted, pastel colored walls, which were hung with several landscape paintings. It was beautiful, and they had achieved a fantastic bargain in buying it.

After an outdoor inspection, the couple took their boat out onto the lake, staying out until twilight, making sure that they docked the boat before dark. Motoring far out onto the lake and along the shores, they discovered that there were two filling stations on the lake, one with a restaurant and the other sporting a general store and a cafe with a bar. The boat was wonderful, and they looked forward to many hours of pleasure with it, boating, water skiing, and, above all, fishing – and sharing their cabin and boat with their relatives and friends.

They spent a glorious night in love-making, talking about their new cabin and the beautiful area of the lake but, mostly about how fortunate they have been that God arranged for them to meet, was providing for them, and was escorting them into a heavenly future filled with love, beauty and pleasure.

The following Friday evening, they drove over to Jesse's to stay overnight, then early in the morning, after Maureen served them a light breakfast, the three of them left for the lake. They drove directly to their cabin, stopping only at a bait store to purchase some bait. While Molly showed her father to his room, Charlie got the boat ready and retrieved all their fishing gear from the shed.

By the time Charlie had the boat ready to go, Molly, a picnic basket, and a beaming Jesse, complete with fishing gear, were all prepared. Charlie drove the boat out to a promising cove which he had previously had his eye on; they fished for about six hours, with only a lunch break, without ever leaving the boat. In the waning afternoon, they returned triumphantly to the cabin with a large catch of fish. Half went to The Amish House, and half the weekend's catch went home to Maureen. Their bounty was abundant, in so many ways.

During the next eight weeks, they spent five weekends at the cabin, going alone twice and taking guests with them three times, including Amos, his wife and his children, Andrew and Clive, who loved every moment of their outdoor lifestyle. They enjoyed their two times alone, much more, by far, than the times in which they had guests. Their love for each other was still so intense that they sought every opportunity to be completely unguarded in their intimacy with each other. In late November, they winterized the cabin and boat, pulled the boat out of the water, and up the ramp into it covered storage place on the dock. They didn't return again until the following March.

During the next month and a half, the couple was very busy. They celebrated both Thanksgiving and Christmas at Jesse's home, and went to a New Year's Eve party at George's place. They also visited Muriel and the children several times during the holiday period. Thanksgiving at Jesse's featured a large roasted turkey with all the trimmings. Maureen did most of the cooking honors, with Molly contributing home-made noodles and biscuits, having watched their preparation at The Amish House. Pumpkin and mincemeat pies, and a fruit salad, were enjoyed as desserts. There were nine people for dinner, and after eating there was a special party to celebrate the announcement that Maureen and her widower, James, would be getting married in three weeks at their church. It was a very nice wedding with two receptions - the first one, with refreshments, was held at the church and the second one was held at Jesse's house, with a potluck dinner and with Molly serving as hostess. Molly noticed the difference from her own wedding to Charlie, of course, but was simply glad that everyone had accepted it by now.

As the holidays approached, Charlie and Molly were unable to decide whether they should do any Christmas decorations. They finally decided to put up a few evergreen wreaths, and to see if Muriel would agree to let them put up a Christmas tree, with all the trimmings, at her mother's house for the children. Betty readily agreed, and on the 20th they took a very nice tree, which they cut down themselves at a nearby Christmas tree farm, along with a great variety of trimmings to Betty's house. Charlie and Roger set up the tree, and they then had an old-fashioned trimming party with Muriel, Roger, and Charlie's oldest daughter, Detty, doing most of the work.

Molly also helped a lot, with Betty mainly taking care of the baby, Brenda, and Charlie playing with the twins, Char and Charlie. Before leaving they left Christmas presents under the tree for Betty, Muriel, Roger and the four children. They also gave Betty a large cured ham, for their Christmas dinner. They arrived back at Betty's home just at sunset on Christmas Eve, and enjoyed watching the children open their presents. Betty served coffee, cocoa, brownies and Christmas cookies, and Muriel surprised Charlie and Molly by introducing them formally to Harry, also known as Dr Manson. Charlie and Molly stayed for about two hours, and then excused themselves to drive to Jesse's house to spend Christmas Eve and day with him, James and Maureen.

To round out their first holiday season, and a very busy one at that, the couple went to the New Year's Eve party at George's. There were four other couples, and six other single people attending the party. It was a very nice party, at which George served Tom-and-Jerry eggnogs, several kinds of wine, a large selection of beers and ales, and about a dozen different kinds of hors d'oeuvres. He also had several bottles of excellent champagne for the New Year's toast after midnight. For the non-drinkers, like Charlie, he served hot cocoa, apple cider and lemonade, and a sparkling cider for the mid-night toast. Everyone had a very good time and Molly was especially pleased to see that George spent a lot of time talking to Charlie

'Happy New Year, darling wife,' whispered Charlie as they clinked glasses at midnight. They didn't kiss, to spare George's feelings.

'I don't see how it could be happier than last year.' Molly tweaked Charlie's fingers. 'I feel as though we've been so lucky that we ought to start sharing it around.'

Charlie smiled, looking thoughtful. 'That's a very Amish approach.'

'How perfect,' said Molly.

It had been a very busy and eventful holiday season, and they looked forward with great happiness to their life together in the coming year, and for many years beyond.

One day at lunch in The Amish House, after a happy weekend of fishing and eating fine fare, Jesse pulled a paper from his pocket and passed it to Molly. It was the part of his will that he made a year before her first marriage, which deeded his property to her, with the stipulation that she live in the home, and take care of him until his death. He had made the will at the time she quit her job to take care of him, after her mother died.

She passed the paper to Charlie, while Jesse cleared his throat.

'I have new proposal for you. Would you and Charlie move into the home and take care of me in my dotage? In return, you'll receive the title to the property.'

Charlie was intrigued, not only because it was a nice, four-acre piece of property with a large house, but also because it contained a barn, numerous outbuildings, a one-acre orchard, and another one-acre piece of ground which had, for years, been used as a very productive garden. His thoughts immediately harkened back to his youth and working on his family's farm and to Wendell's family sharecropping on the property.

The memory of his own family's sense of charity returned to him. 'We'll do all that for you, Jesse, you know we will. But you don't have to deed us the farm.'

'Let us have a think about it, Dad, and get back to you.'

'Well, be quick as you can,' said Jesse, tucking into a slice of apple pie. 'I'm not getting younger any time soon.'

For the next two months, they pondered the pluses and minuses of Jesse's proposal. They had already been trying to decide whether they would continue to rent the home they were in, or find a nice home to purchase. Jesse's proposal forced them to finally get serious about it.

Near the end of the two-month period, their first anniversary rolled around. They spent the entire time at the cabin as a repeat of their honeymoon at the lake. As promised, they devoted a lot of time to discussing Jesse's proposal. In the end, they easily decided that they would conditionally accept Jesse's offer and move into his home, as soon as possible. Living in a large house on a farm - albeit a mini-farm - fulfilled Charlie's most frequent dream while he was in prison.

Furthermore, they were certain that they could easily take care of Jesse, no matter how long he lived and no matter what his future needs might be. He was nearing the end of his term of office and had decided not to run for re-election as County Sheriff, and regardless of how much longer he worked he would retire within a few years, in reasonably good health and fitness. Molly would be retiring within the next six years, or so, at which time she would have all her time to devote to caring for the property and her father. To put the icing on the cake, they decided to have the property appraised and pay Jesse the full value in cash (from George's settlement on Molly), to be put into savings or investments that he could bequest from his estate. Without hesitation, he accepted the general outlines of the plan, and gave them permission to proceed with it as soon as possible.

They began immediately to plan remodelling and refurbishment, and when Jesse worried about the fees involved, Molly finally told him about George's gifts to her and Charlie. His worries settled, Jesse hired local painters, carpenters and craftsmen and had them all working before the end of the week. By the end of the first month, the workers had completed most of the work on the exterior of the house, and on the mini-farm itself. The crowning jewel of the modifications was the beautiful bluegrass lawn which had been sodded around the house, and set-off by a pretty white picket fence. They also enclosed the one-acre garden with a four-foot high chain-link fence, to protect it from the animals which would be roaming about the farm.

It took the better part of three months to complete everything inside the house itself. The most time-consuming projects were the modernization of the kitchen and bathroom, which were both fitted with brand-new fixtures and appliances; the building of a three-bedroom apartment, complete with dining room, kitchen and bathroom, in the huge basement, and the conversion of the attic into a bedroom with its own bathroom. The back one-third of the basement was remodeled into a very large pantry, with shelving and bins for food storage. The house was also brought up to modern building codes with new electrical wiring, plumbing pipes, and heating/cooling ductwork.

After getting everything moved into their new home and vacating their rental home, they went shopping for a new car, deciding on purchasing a mid-size, beige-colored Buick, with a brown and beige interior. They had everything they needed and more, and continually expressed their gratitude for such blessings.

Once the remodeling and construction were completed, and they were settled into their new home, they decided to begin spending weekends at their lake house. Moreover, they decided to make the first weekend a celebratory one, with Jesse as their guest, relaxing and fishing at their cabin, and seeing their friends and having meals at the Amish House

They were still only early into their second year of marriage, but somehow they had gathered friends and family around them and acquired a four-acre "mini-farm". Nearly every other weekend was spent at their lake cabin, even during the winter, now that it was heated with their wonderful wood-burning stove.

On the weekends that they didn't use their cabin, they did their best to make sure it was used by relatives and friends. Betty, Muriel, and Muriel's second husband, Dr. Harold Manson (Harry). They had married before Charlie's and Molly's first wedding anniversary, and used the cabin frequently, usually taking the children with them. Johnny and his wife used it often, too, and Amos, Annie and the boys were regular visitors. Even George used it several times, after turning down many earlier invitations.

Things went well with their work at the factory. Molly received two more raises before she retired, while Charlie was promoted from Assistant Manager to Manager of the factory's tool and supply rooms, and procurement department. Their incomes continued to increase up to their retirements, and even after Muriel re-married, since they were used to living without Charlie's income, they opened a savings account for each of the children's college or professional education.

They saw Charlie's children several times a month, often having them out to the "farm". Because of the size of the house and the many things to do outside, they very much loved visiting their parents. A year after the construction and remodeling were complete, they had a very nice playground constructed between the barn and the garden, and with quite a menagerie of animals running around, the kids loved it.

The years passed. The children grew. Their love intensified. After a few more years, they were invited by their beloved friends at The Amish House to join in for the wedding of the young Amish folk they had watched grow up, and it was something they were privileged to share many times over.

Their cup of love was truly full, so much so that it completely ran over, and they remembered, over and over, how blessed they were, and how they should let those blessings be shared with others.

Chapter 20

In God's Garden

I come to the garden alone, while the dew is still on the roses,
And the voice I hear, falling on my ear, the Son of God discloses.
And He walks with me, and He talks with me,
and He tells me I am His own,
And the joy we share as we tarry there, none other has ever known.

In the Garden, C. Austin Miles

They continued to remodel and rebuild things over the years, including the lake house which they extended comprehensively with the help of Paul, their Amish builder. Molly retired after twenty years at the factory, followed by Charlie at the age of fifty-eight, with both in fine health that they attributed to robust lifestyles on the mini-farm and the lake, and their love for God's creation, all of God's creatures, and especially each other.

By the time the happy couple completed their lake home, they had also lived on their mini-farm for twenty-five years. The young fruit trees they'd planted in their orchard were five years old and beginning to bear harvestable fruit. In another five years, the trees would reach maximum production. Their orchard, like their vegetable garden, was not just highly productive – it was a beautiful sight to see. Over the years, they had increased the fertility and productivity of the farm's soil, especially in the vegetable garden, through heavy annual additions of compost and manure, and they tended the farm's plants with expert management and tender loving care.

For the garden, they did their best to procure seeds and plantings of the best, tastiest varieties of vegetables available, maintaining their health by using natural, biological control of pestiferous insects and diseases, taking advantage across the farm of the free advice provided by the US Department of Agriculture and services provided by the University Agricultural Extension offices.

Eventually, they began working with several garden clubs and organized share-cropping, which enabled them to divide their time between the farm and lake house, as they could leave it in the care of Frank and June, their dear neighbors, friends and share-cropping partners.

In essence, Charlie was applying all the 4-H principles that he had been learning at the age of fifteen – only now he was free and doing it all on his own farm, sharing the experience with the love of his life.

Of course, as the years flew by they witnessed their share of tragedy and loss. Muriel's brother was lost in action in Vietnam, and because their father was still in prison he wasn't allowed to attend the memorial service. Cecil was eventually to die in prison, having never been paroled. Betty, Muriel's mother, died in her seventies, as did Maureen, Molly's beloved sister. Tommy died during the eighties of a disease which reduced him to skin and bone and from which he appeared to have just wasted away, and then at the age of 79, Molly and Charlie lost their dear friend - and Molly's former husband - George. Jesse suffered a stroke and was incapacitated so that he needed a great deal of Molly's attention.

Their friends began to disappear around them, but they always had each other and, of course, their loving children who adored them throughout, even calling Molly 'Aunt Molly' as encouraged by Muriel, and then eventually their children's children, and the offspring of their friends and neighbors who they gathered around them like crops growing toward sunlight. They put all their kids through college, apart from Charlie III who chose the armed forces instead, and then they set about assisting their grandchildren, not just with financial means, but by shining like a great light ahead of them, tilling the land with hoes for excellent exercise, sharing the bounties of their growing programs, inviting them to the lake house and the mini-farm to share in all they'd achieved.

When staying at their farm house, they were usually constantly busy with work, mostly outside with the garden and tending to the animals. Because they were acquiring more and more Amish attire, they began to routinely wear the very durable and serviceable clothing, shoes and boots, when working around the farm. Made of natural fibers that were grown organically on Amish or Mennonite farms, and creatively hand-woven on Amish-made looms, the clothing kept the wearer cooler in summer and warmer in winter than typical factory-manufactured clothing. The shoes and boots were also super comfortable, as well as durable, made of leathers from locally grown animals which was hand-tanned by Amish professionals, and custom-made by the hands of Amish experts in leather and artisans in shoe making.

While they were living in their lake home they ate out a great deal, but they rarely did when living in their farm home. Nearly all the food they ate while there was grown or raised on their farm, and nearly all their meals were prepared by Molly. Molly loved to cook and bake, to the enormous delight of Charlie, who absolutely loved to have the home flooded with the mouth-watering aromas of baked foods, especially biscuits - and she spent hours each day in creating delicious meals and snacks for her and Charlie, as well as their many guests and visitors.

It seemed that they almost always had at least one other person eating with them at every meal of the day. With neighborhood children, and grandchildren, around most of the time, sometimes quite a few of them running in and out of the house, Molly kept the kitchen and dining room tables loaded with breads, biscuits, pies, cakes, cookies, donuts, jams and jellies, a variety of seasonal fruits and vegetables, and other snacks. She also made sure that the coffee pots were kept filled with fresh coffee, the teapot ready to brew tea, and the refrigerators filled with pitchers of milk, cider, and water, as well as with lunch meats, cheeses, and other delectable snacks, such as home-made candies. On most days, it seemed, there was a steady stream of children, and adults, grabbing items from the tables and refrigerators, and either eating them on the run, or sitting, singly or in small groups, at a table.

The house pantries were kept fully stocked with condiments, home-grown herbs, a variety of flour and other baking and cooking ingredients, a variety of canned fruits and vegetables (mostly contained in Mason jars), and baskets of a variety of fruits and vegetables. The cellar shelves were literally full of canned fruits; vegetables; fruit sauces, jams and jellies; slabs and rounds of cheeses, and many other delectable food items; the cellar floor was crammed with crocks, kegs, and large jars of ciders, juices, beers and milk, and baskets of fruit and vegetables; and hanging from crossbeams of the cellar ceiling, were cured hams and large tubes of thuringers, sausages and other processed meats.

From the time she was a girl, helping her mother in the kitchen, Molly became quite experienced in canning and other forms of food preservation. However, she did not even come close to having the experience, skills and creativity of June, their share-cropper.

To Molly, June seemed to be as good if not better than any of the Amish food preservers she'd met. She had, infrequently, done some canning with June, mostly vegetables from their garden such as tomatoes, green beans, shelly beans, corn, beets, and pickles.

However, once they completed renovating their lake home, she began to get more serious about it, and every year thereafter, she and June preserved hundreds and hundreds of jars of vegetables, fruits, tomato juice, apple butter, apple sauce, jams and jellies, mostly during three month periods from mid-August through mid-November. Although Molly became quite skilled at it, and had acquired all the necessary cookers, pots, pans, Mason jars, rubber gaskets, lids, jelly jars and sealing paraffin wax, she always canned with June - either in her kitchen or in June's. In fact, Frank built his wife an annex to their kitchen specifically for canning, which, when completed, they used almost exclusively for their joint canning projects.

As they continued to increase the fertility of the garden and orchard, they became increasingly productive - especially when the fruit trees grew to maturity. Eventually it reached the point where they simply could not eat or can all of it, so they then had the great pleasure of giving large proportions of the fruits and vegetables, and even canned goods, to their many relatives, friends and neighbors. Charlie and Molly had always been generous with the fruits of their farm, but now they had to actively encourage people to accept a substantial part of their harvests, to keep the excesses from rotting in the field. Fortunately, there was enough hauled away by grateful recipients that nothing produced on the farm ever went to waste.

Charlie discussed all of this with his Amish friends, and discovered that they regularly used services provided by the USDA and county agricultural agents, even though the agencies viewed Amish agricultural practices as nineteenth century and archaic. The Amish weren't bothered about the views of outside communities, preferring to build from within with a constant drive among farmers, blacksmiths and craftsmen to improve their way of life by incorporating new ideas. Charlie and Molly adored that way of life, and became quite expert in Amish ways, Charlie working with the carpenters and Molly noodle-making and baking in the kitchens at the barn raisings they attended.

Then at their thirtieth wedding anniversary, over at the lake, Charlie surprised Molly with a horse, a beautiful black mare (which Molly named Black Beauty) to pull along the buggy which they borrowed from their old friend Aaron from time to time. They dearly loved to take buggy rides behind the fast-paced trotting of Black Beauty, through the peaceful Amish rural landscape, and to visit the many quaint small towns scattered about the beautiful countryside…

'Hang on there a moment,' I said, leaning forward to distract Luther from his fascinating tale.

We had sat by the lake, and then in my little square cabin, for the best part of nine hours as he'd related the histories of the people in the cabin next door, the ones he called his great aunt and uncle. I had seen them return to their grand lake house, laughing, flushed by the wind as they'd driven along in their open-air buggy. Luther had popped across to tell them where he was, and they'd waved to me briefly before heading into the house. Minutes later I'd heard the unmistakeable sound of logs being split as Charlie – or perhaps Molly – prepared the open fire for the evening.

It had grown dark without me noticing, so I took advantage of the break I'd created in the conversation to jump up and turn on the light. It glared uncompromisingly on the lids of the four beer bottles we'd managed to sink between us. It had been a long day, mind you, and we'd punctuated it with little meals from Luther's backpack, stocked as it was with all varieties of snacks and goodies. Now I'd heard all about their growing and canning activities, I could guess where it was all from.

Luther smiled at me patiently. 'You have a question?'

'Questions, more like.' I counted them out on my fingers. 'So that couple next door, Henry Fonda and Katherine Hepburn.' I could see Luther didn't understand the Golden Pond reference, so I powered on. 'They're seventy years old?'

'A little more, I think,' replied Luther.

'And they've been married for thirty odd years. And a bit more. But he was a bank robber who served time for two whole decades from the age of fifteen, and she was married to a gay sheriff who clearly died of Aids, followed by an impotent confirmed bachelor who contributed to both their divorces. Is that right?'

Luther frowned. 'Well, he was only the driver at the bank robbery,' he said carefully, as if to an idiot. His expression was along the lines of: 'That was a fundamental point. How much more have you missed?'

'And they were adopted into a large Amish community and, therefore have a massive family of people, none of whom are actually related to them?'

'Precisely,' said Luther, apparently satisfied that I'd learned my lesson well. He did a good Obe Wan Kenobi impression. 'So those are really just repetitions of what I've just told you.'

'Confirmations,' I corrected him. 'Important to get your facts straight in journalism.'

He raised his eyebrows. 'Okay. Then what's your actual question?'

Ha. Somehow this young man had a way of making me feel brainless. He'd be a good reporter – or maybe a politician – if he chose to go in that direction.

'Well, your story has just come right up to date, to the barn-raising and the horse pulling the buggy, and you wanting to know if I like to drive fast. So I guess I'm wondering—'

'Where do I fit in?' Luther smiled knowingly, and I had the feeling that he'd been quite aware what my question was going to be from the second I stopped him. A lawyer, then. Maybe he'd be a lawyer. Maybe he already was a lawyer.

'Exactly,' I said.

'Andrew is my father,' he told me, waving a hand at the lakeside. 'I've been coming here for holidays for as long as I can remember, and I've known Molly and Charlie all my life.'

'Andrew? I don't remember Andrew.'

There'd been a lot of names, to be fair, and my pen had run out after the Second World War section so most of this was being committed to a fast-fading memory.

'There was a name starting with A, though. Amos,' I remembered. 'Amos! They remained friends and Charlie got him the job in the payroll office.'

Luther smiled again, as if I'd passed his test. 'Yep. Amos was my grandfather, and Charlie was his brother. That's why I call him Great Uncle Charlie.'

'Amos *was* ...' I probed gently for fear of what he might have to say.

'He died a couple of years ago,' said Luther. 'Aneurism. He always liked to say he had too many brains for one head.'

'I'm sorry to hear that. Did he stay at the factory like Charlie and Molly?'

'He certainly did,' said Luther proudly. 'He became the company accountant in the end, and retired on a decent pension at the age of sixty-five. Got the gold watch and everything,' he added, drawing back his sleeve so that I could see it on his arm. 'Dad let me wear it so I could show it to Uncle Charlie. He's been so busy since Amos died that he hadn't seen it.'

'Wow,' I said. 'Extraordinary.'

It really was extraordinary – the whole story.

Then I remembered another question. 'So why did you ask me if I like to drive fast?'

The moment I asked it, I realized I could have answered that particular query for myself.

'It's what Charlie asks all the young folks he gets to know,' said Luther. 'It's what he asked me when I turned sixteen. Charlie was always a fast driver, always loved the open road and his foot to the floor, but he knew – he *learned* – that you have to keep it under control. And sometimes, when you're fifteen or sixteen, you don't know so much about keeping it under control.'

'Did you?'

Luther laughed. 'I like a fast car as much as the next man,' he said, 'but I believe the other things that Molly and Charlie have always stood for are more valuable. Learning and education, firstly. Living lightly on the land. Taking personal responsibility for your actions – and loving until there's enough to spread around. I took it all seriously and became an accountant. Like my grandfather.'

'Those are pretty good values,' I said with a smile.

'And redemption,' added Luther suddenly. 'Uncle Charlie has always believed in second chances. He reckoned that

God gave him several – avoiding the chair, learning so much in prison, getting paroled, his wonderful children …'

'And Molly,' I finished for him.

Luther didn't say anything, but his smile spoke volumes.

We paused, staring out over the lake as the cool breeze ruffled its surface into foamy waves. Sitting here, with the calm blackness of the water ahead of us and the rustle of the trees behind, it was easy to believe in redemption. In all of it, in fact.

'Hey,' I said to Luther as he handed me another beer, 'do you think I could meet them?'

He checked his grandfather's gold watch, then pulled a face. 'It's quite late. I don't think they'll want to be disturbed.' And he gave me a slow, deliberate wink.

'Really? At seventy plus?'

'Love until there's enough to spread around,' he repeated.

We both laughed, and took a slug of our beer.

Chapter 21

Together Again

Don't you think that everyone looks back on their childhood with certain amounts of bitterness and regret? It doesn't have to ruin your life!

Ethel, On Golden Pond

I didn't hear from Luther for many years, long after I'd broken down the story and sold it to my editor as the most interesting tale he would ever hear of things we'd all thought were going to be boring. I sectioned it down into its component parts, researched it more thoroughly, and managed to parlay it into four or five different features focusing on Vanity Fair articles about the infamous bank robbers of the thirties, the prisoner squads in the military services, the incidence of Aids among the police force. Somehow the tale of Amish progress never made it into print.

I always felt it was a shame that I hadn't gotten to meet Charlie and Molly. They'd left for the mini-farm by the time I emerged from my cabin the next day, slightly jaded from the beer and my extended concentration on Luther's story. Besides, I got the feeling from Luther that they would have eschewed any focus on them as protagonists in my column or a feature. They just believed in making the most of what they had, like anybody would in their shoes – so they thought.

Almost two decades later, however, I received an email from one Luther Bendon, CFO at a multi-national manufacturing company in Denver, saying:

Dear Brendon,

I know this will be a bolt from the blue. It's been a long time since our lakeside discussion about my great aunt and uncle, Molly and Charlie.

Aunt Molly died just a few days ago. Her funeral is going to be held at the end of the week at the mini-farm, and I thought you might like to attend. Uncle Charlie died nine years ago, and Molly's been running the farm herself since then.

Give me a call if you'd like to come along. I'm sure you'd find it interesting to see how it all turned out.

Best wishes,

Luther

I reached for my phone immediately.

Luther met me at the airport, shaking my hand warmly. He looked exactly the same, apart from some white dusting to his hair, while I looked and felt like I wouldn't be long after Aunt Molly, particularly after a five-hour flight.

He led me to his car, a rather impressive BMW.

'Do you like to drive fast?' I asked him wryly, and he grinned.

'Yes, I do,' he said, 'and now I can – but only at the race track when I pay for a lesson.'

We settled into the car, and Luther filled me in on what had happened.

Later in life, Molly and Charlie had purchased a holiday home on an estate in Florida, where the weather was warmer for their joints and the community like-minded and convivial. One evening they were playing hand-and-foot (a version of their beloved canasta) at a neighbor's, two doors away, where they and the three other couples had provided a dish for a pot-luck supper. They'd had an incredible night, and couldn't remember every playing so well.

As they departed, carrying their dishes, Charlie almost fell on the porch steps. He caught himself, but after a few steps on the neighbor's flagstone walkway, he tripped and fell into the darkness beyond the area lit by the porch-light. The casserole dish slipped from his hands, shattering noisily against the doorway, and Charlie, whose legs were often numb because of his diabetes, struck his head very hard on the rocks of a raised-bed flower garden.

Molly flew immediately to his side, kneeling, trying to find out what had happened. When she was unable to rouse him, a feeling of dread began to creep over her. Soon the others were at her side; one of them called the emergency services while others brought a blanket, a pillow, a flashlight. When they lifted his head onto the pillow, there was a large pool of blood where his head had lain. Several of the friends were attempting to hear a heartbeat, feel a pulse or rouse Charlie by talking to him. Molly's feeling of dread intensified. Without knowing, she began swaying her body and humming some of Charlie's favorite tunes.

Her reverie was soon starkly interrupted by the sound of sirens and a stirring of activity of the people around her, causing her to instinctively lean over and lay her head on her lover's chest. At about the same time, the area was flooded with a glare of flashing red lights from the arriving ambulance. As soon as the ambulance came to a stop, the emergency crew rushed to Charlie's side with a gurney, lifted him onto it, and then quickly wheeled him to the ambulance.

Molly was guided to a chair beside the gurney in the back of the ambulance, which immediately sped off with lights flashing and sirens blaring, to the emergency entrance of the hospital. As they careened down the road, she watched as they worked on her husband, preparing him for the nurses and doctors at the hospital. The fact that they were working on him gave her hope that he was still alive, and would be saved at the hospital. However, in her heart she was filled with dread that he was gone.

After coming to a sudden stop at the hospital's emergency entrance, Charlie's gurney was quickly removed and rushed through the doors. Molly was assisted out of the ambulance and slowly walked into the emergency room toward the receiving desk. She was in a fog, feeling light-headed, and beginning to wobble on her feet. Fortunately, before she fainted, she was grabbed on both sides and guided to a chair.

As she was being seated she began slowly to become aware that every one of the people they'd played cards with was with her. Molly's niece, Harriet, and her husband, Hank, who lived nearby, were also there. She was glad to see all of them. She was especially pleased to have Harriet there, as she relieved her of filling out all the forms which she was being asked to sign.

Before long, a doctor came to give her the news which she was dreading to hear: the love of her life was dead. Her soul mate of over forty-five years had left her at the young age of only 84. The doctor told her that he was pronounced dead on arrival. He had severely fractured his skull when he fell, which had immediately rendered him unconscious. The doctor assured her that he'd been completely unconscious. He did not suffer as he passed away.

Life went on, as it always does for the living, and especially for Molly who was determined not to give in to depression and old age. She was surprised by how much she enjoyed the company of her friends. She was still able to drive, and everyone offered to help around the farm, so the practical things would be taken care of, for now at least.

What could never be taken care of was the hole in her life left by Charlie. She organized his funeral with the help of the children and June, who had become more family than friend, paying close attention to the gravesite, and especially the tombstone.

It was a beautiful double tombstone. At the top, their surname was engraved in large letters. Beneath it, Charlie's name and lifespan were carved into the left side, over his grave, and on the right side was her name, with enough space underneath to add the dates of her lifespan once her body was laid in the grave next to her husband.

Finally, at the bottom of the stone were two arms – a larger, masculine one, reaching up from the left, clasping the hand of a smaller, feminine one which curved up from the right. She thought of the appropriateness of the clasped hands, because Charlie had always held her hand whenever they walked together.

'I'm so sad you were taken from me, Charlie, at such a young age, and in such a brutal way,' she'd whispered at the graveside. His goal had been to live as long as his grandfather, who was just a few days shy of his 100th birthday when he died. 'But I will live with your spirit always by my side, until I eventually join you in Heaven.'

She promised to visit their gravesite as often as she could, but at least once a month. Finally, she knelt on his grave and kissed his name, and their hands, on the tombstone. And then she stood, brushed down her dress, and set about organizing a life for the living.

Charlie would have wanted that.

We'd arrived at the church, at the edge of the graveyard where Molly was to be buried, and the sight was extraordinary. I'd never seen a place of worship so packed. It was as if a major celebrity had died.

Luther introduced me to his wife and daughter, and then to Molly's niece who had helped her with the forms when Charlie died. 'You go on,' I said to him as his wife began to look distressed. 'I can work it out all out for myself.'

'Did you know my aunt?' asked Harriet, the niece.

'Only by her glorious reputation.'

Harriet laughed. 'Well, she would have liked to hear that, I think.' She led me toward a pew and then asked, 'Can I tell you who anyone is?'

'Who are all the vets?' I asked, amazed to see so many uniformed men and women greeting each other with an ease and familiarity that spoke of close friendship.

'Yet more adopted family.' Harriet watched my face as I tried to process yet another extension to this enormous brood, and smiled at my confusion. 'Several years before Molly began living alone, Charlie III, a 20-yr veteran of the Marine Corps, and his brother-in-law, Michael, a 20-yr veteran of the Army, founded an American Legion Post not far from the mini-farm. They wanted to help needy veterans, especially the ones who were homeless.'

'Extraordinary,' I said again. This couple were the gift that just kept on giving.

'Indeed. Do you know anybody to sit with?'

I looked around the room, and somehow I felt like I knew everybody. Although the characters and people Luther had told me about would be gone, here were their offspring and other halves and legacies. Here would be their children, their grandchildren, their friends and their children, the formidable share-cropper June, and perhaps even the Amish youngsters who had married with the help of Charlie and Molly.

I hunched my shoulders. 'Not really,' I said, 'but I'll just sit here at the back, if I may.'

'Sure,' said Harriet, and bustled away to deal with some other waif and stray who was wandering around, looking lost.

I parked myself beside a family of five, who smiled at me with huge welcoming grins although they'd never met me before in my life.

'Brendon,' I said, by way of introduction.

The woman pointed to her left. 'This is my husband, Prentice,' she said, 'and I'm Jemima. These are our grandchildren, Ruby, Rebecca and Martin.'

The children, who ranged between about ten and fifteen or so, all shook my hand solemnly.

'Did you know Molly well?' asked Jemima.

I shook my head. 'Hardly at all, unfortunately. How about you?'

'She saved our lives,' said Prentice, as Jemima's eyes filled with tears.

Here we go, I thought, and as the crowds continued to pour in, I heard their story.

When Molly became a little more infirm (she'd been eighty-five when Charlie died, after all), she had made a small concession in her manner of living: she agreed to hire a live-in housekeeper.

She was introduced to Jemima, and liked her from the start. Fortunately, Jemima was immediately available to provide weekly maid service and Molly hired her on the spot. Over the next few weeks they discovered not only that Jemima was an excellent housekeeper, but was also a grandmother of three and married to Prentice, a 20-year veteran of the Navy, who retired as Chief Petty Office, and was a long-term employee of the U.S. Postal Service.

They lived in a small, three-bedroom home on the edge of the shabbiest, most crime-ridden area of the city. She and Prentice had been raising their three grandchildren for the past seven years, since their daughter died of a drug overdose. It had been quite a struggle, mainly because they were stuck in a neighborhood that not only was extremely dangerous, but also offered only a dismal future for the children. It was literally impossible for them protect the children from daily exposure to drugs, prostitution, pornography, profane music and language, robbery, shootings, and murder.

Worst of all, in their opinion, were the public schools the children were forced to attend, which left the children so poorly prepared in the three R's that most of them were essentially unqualified for anything except the lowest paying jobs in society. As soon as the children began attending their local elementary school, they began to become increasingly desperate to find a way to move the children to a better environment.

So when Jemima discovered that the basement apartment at Molly's house had never been lived in and wasn't likely to be any time soon, she immediately made a proposal to Molly. Her proposal was simple and straight-forward: she would keep the house cleaned, inside and out, do the laundry, and do the cooking for her and her guests, and her family would do the maintenance, landscaping, and other chores of the farm. Her family would basically take care of everything in the house, and on the farm, and their only compensation would be a lease on the basement apartment. Jemima reasoned that Molly would essentially be getting all her skilled labor for free, since the apartment was not being rented, nor were there plans to rent it in the future. Molly readily agreed with Jemima's proposal, and told her that she would immediately have the lease drawn up by her attorney.

Jemima was so overjoyed that she could hardly wait to surprise Prentice with the good news. After finishing her day's work, and thanking Molly so profusely that it embarrassed her, Jemima left for home, literally shaking with excitement.

As she rushed into her home, sobbing uncontrollably, Prentice ran to her side, thinking that she had met with a tragedy.

After controlling her sobs, she told him excitedly about their new home. Although he had never seen the house, nor the mini-farm, Jemima had described it in glowing terms many times. When the children heard shouts of 'Bless the Lord' and 'Hallelujah' and 'We've been delivered', they ran into the room to stand at her side and the group stood for a long time in a five-way hug.

Over a celebratory supper at McDonald's, Jemima described the brand-new apartment where they would be living.

'It's on a farm,' she told them. 'A fresh green farm with many, many animals, and a vegetable garden, and fruit that you can pick in the orchard straight from the trees, and you will be encouraged to do just that! There's lots of wonderful fresh air, and best of all, there are amazing, safe schools for you to attend, all three of you. It's truly a miracle.'

And shortly after arriving back at their home, the miracle improved. Jemima received a phone call from Molly telling her that she would have the lease ready for signing the next day. The family could begin moving in as early as tomorrow. She also told her that her neighbor had several trucks had volunteered to help with the move.

As soon as Prentice left for work, Jemima loaded her car with some of the family's personal belongings, dropped the three children off at their school, and then made a bee-line to the farm. Molly was on the porch as she drove up and parked, and invited her to come into the dining room for coffee and pie. As soon as she sat down at the table, a smiling Molly shoved the lease over to her for her to sign. Jemima signed it without even reading it, trusting Molly and her attorney, implicitly.

'Welcome to you and your family,' said Molly, gripping Jemima's hand. 'I'm so happy about it, and I know it will mean an enriched future for us all.'

Before leaving, Jemima took the personal items she'd brought with her to the apartment and carried out a quick survey of its layout and contents. She had been in the apartment several times before, to dust and vacuum, but had not remembered how it was laid out.

Now she could see that it had three bedrooms, a bathroom, a kitchen/dining room combination, and a living room. Each bedroom had a large closet, a queen-sized bed, and a dresser, and the kitchen was furnished with a refrigerator, range and dishwasher, and the apartment was heated and cooled by a combination furnace and air conditioner, contained in a utility room, along with the hot-water tank. It was altogether a substantially larger and better arranged than the house they had been living in. She made a decision to give the largest bedroom to the girls, while the smallest would go to Martin, and the medium-sized one would be occupied by her and Prentice.

Two days later they made their move, with June's son Norm and his oldest son providing one of their trucks as well as their labor. The move took less than half a day to complete. The children had already been enrolled in their new school, and the owner of their rental home notified. They were so desperate to get the children away from their hellish environment that they paid the rent up to the end of the 30-day notice without hesitation, even though they would not be living in it.

As they settled in, the extended family lived very harmoniously and happily together, to the great benefit of each one of them, including Molly and her family who knew she was well looked after.

From the first day of living on the farm, until their dying day, all five members of the family would thank their lucky stars. Jemima and Prentice were happy beyond words. The children had never looked back, responding to their new environment and opportunities with such gratitude, joy and enthusiasm that they propelled themselves through the educational system with high academic achievement and honors. From the beginning, they loved their school and their teachers, and responded to living on the farm like baby ducks taking to water.

Jemima turned out to be even a better housekeeper and cook than Molly had imagined, while Prentice proved to be an exceptionally responsible and skilled handyman about the farm.

Moreover, Jemima volunteered to cook, do the laundry, and clean their rooms for the homeless veterans. Prentice had already joined the American Legion Post, so he volunteered to supervise the veterans living on the farm. He would see that they not only were provided with room and board, but also with therapeutic work, helping to care for the farm's animals, garden and orchard. A program bonus was that June's family hired many of the veterans for part-time and even full-time employment in their expanding share-cropping, organic-produce business. Eventually, there were as many as a dozen homeless veterans living on the farm at any one time, keeping Jemima and Prentice very busy. Molly's care and generosity of the homeless veterans' program continued even after her death, when she left much of the residue of her estate - a substantial amount - to the American Legion Post, specifically dedicated to the program,

And that wasn't all she'd bequeathed to others. In Molly's will, she'd provided for college educations for each of her new 'great-grandchildren' – Jemima and Prentice's grandchildren. Not only that, but to the great surprise of Jemima and Prentice, she had extended the lease on their apartment until the end of their lives. It was the least she could do for such dear friends, she'd told her attorney ...

It was Jemima who'd found Molly, at the end. Apparently, Molly had suffered from heart fibrillation episodes and high blood pressure. At the age of 95, she had the most serious episode of all and needed to be hospitalized, but they managed to stabilize her and sent her home. Over the next few days, she remained in a relatively stable condition.

It was late October, and the area was experiencing one of the nicest Indian Summers in memory. Molly decided to visit Charlie at the grave. She had lunch in town with Jemima and family, and some other friends, then went home to take a nap before dinner.

She arose after an hour and put on Charlie's favorite dress: a white silk sheath with padded shoulders, beautifully printed with red roses and vivid green leaves. Everyone commented on how nice she looked, and she made a point of hugging everyone, especially her 'new' great grandchildren, Ruby, Becky and Martin. They all enjoyed a fabulous meal, and then Molly excused herself at twilight to take a stroll through the garden before retiring. She placed her gold, tasselled shawl over her shoulders and strolled along the path, steadied by her cane, singing the third stanza of her favorite song, the one she had sung ever since he'd died, as she wandered into the garden, toward the golden light she saw shining in the distance ...

When Molly did not come back into the house at dark, Jemima and Prentice went out to look for her. They couldn't see her from the porch, but noticed the moonbeam shining down on the garden. They walked toward it, flashlights at the ready, and there they found the prostrate Molly, lying on her back in a relaxed state, as if she had lain down to sleep for the night.

After they'd confirmed that she'd passed, and the emergency squad had arrived, the crew and the assembled guests all commented that they were amazed by what they saw as they looked down at Molly. An angelic aura of light radiated from her smiling face, as they gently lifted her away, as if she was greeting someone. Someone she loved very much indeed.

The church was beginning to grow quiet as I heard the end of Jemima's tale. I squeezed her hand in recognition – although quite what I was acknowledging, I didn't know – and turned to face the front, but not before I had caught the eye of Martin, the fifteen-year-old.

I winked at him. 'So, Martin,' I said. 'Do you like to drive fast?'

And I knew by the way he snorted with laughter that he'd heard it before, and he would hear it again until the end of his days, from Charlie whom he'd never met, and the people on whom Charlie and Molly had created such an impression - including one man, a lowly reporter, whom they'd once waved at, but never met face-to-face.

That was his loss, he couldn't help but feel.

Luther met me at the graveside later, once the people in Molly's huge family network had gathered to celebrate her life. I was simply standing, studying the gravestone she'd had designed for herself and Charlie.

'I wish I'd met them that day at the lake,' I said to him, as if he were a dear friend rather than someone with whom I'd once had a conversation. 'I feel as if I know them, but I've been a bit ... cheated, somehow.'

Luther nodded. 'I can see why you'd feel that. That's why I thought you might appreciate these.'

I stared down at the parcel in his hand – a carrier bag, stuffed with pieces of paper of all shapes and sizes, folded roughly into three inch squares. I pulled some out at random: they were written on time cards, invoices, supply requisitions, note pads, clocking-in cards – all manner of company forms and paraphernalia.

'I've cleared it with the family,' said Luther, 'and they agreed you should have them, for the time being, at least.' He nudged my arm. 'I guess you're one of us now.'

'But what is this stuff?' I called as he wound his way past the graveside toward his family.

'It's their love letters. Charlie's and Molly's.' He smiled again, and I remembered his capacity for making me feel dim. 'Over to you now, Brendon. Do something with them.'

I stood there for ages, staring into that bag, looking between the little squares of notes and the grave where Molly now lay, beside her beloved Charlie.

'So, Charlie and Molly,' I said eventually. 'What am I supposed to do with this lot?'

But somehow, I already knew the answer.

The end

*'I'd stay in the garden with Him, tho the night around me be falling,
But He bids me go, through the voice of woe, His voice to me is calling.
And he walks with me and He talks to me, and He tells me I am His own,
And the joy we share as we tarry there, none other has ever known.'*

In the Garden, C. Austin Miles, as sung by Molly

My heart feels heavy now but I know when I see you, the old ache will be gone and I'll be happy again. My heart aches when you are gone, but you should hear it sing when you are near. As I write this little note, I keep wondering if anything may have happened to you. I'm keeping my fingers crossed till I can see you with my own eyes.

Charlie's 44th letter

Acknowledgments

I first want to acknowledge and thank my wife, Freda, who, for the nearly five years it took me to write this novel, not only had the patience of a Saint but also was strongly encouraging during periods when I tired or wavered. Especially during this past year, when I often had papers scattered all over the house, she complained but very little. Her most important contribution, however, was her diligent editing of three of the manuscripts as the novel was transformed from its original expansive, biographical form, into its present concise and lively novel form.

Special kudos goes to the very talented Kelly McKain, the HappyLiving.com editor, who was the designated editor for the original biographical-style manuscript. However, after a thorough reading, she quickly saw its strong potential to be transformed into a powerfully poignant and inspirational love story in the hands of an exceptionally talented novelist. This led, based on Kelly's recommendation, to the serendipitous hiring of Jill Marshall – her friend, fellow editor and neighbor in Surrey, England - to do the honors. I'm sure that readers will agree that Happy Living Books Independent Publishers could not have made a better choice.

I also want to give a special thanks to two friends, Shelley McGlamery and Trina Pruett, who read the original manuscript, and wrote valuable evaluations and recommendations which contributed to important improvements.

I would be remiss in not thanking my granddaughter, Kaileen Elise Sues, for strongly recommending Kelly to edit my manuscript; and in not recognizing, and thanking, my grandson, Kyle Gersper, for supervising the selection of the novel's cover, helping with its marketing, and especially for helping me learn how to edit manuscripts using Microsoft Word.

Last, but not least, I want to express my heart-felt admiration and thanks to the father of Kaileen and Kyle - my son, Matthew Gersper, founder of HappyLiving.com - for believing in me and my project, and agreeing to publish the novel.

Finally, I want to thank the readers of the novel. I hope you enjoy reading it, as much as Jill and I enjoyed writing it. We both hope, especially, that you are inspired by the journey of love and devotion followed by Charlie and Molly.

Sincerely yours, Paul L. Gersper

The Author and the Publisher
In their own words

I love inspiration! It has the power to change lives for the better.

I also love that it's even-handed. It happens to all of humanity: young and old; rich and poor; the 60-hour-per-week city worker and the organic farmer; employers and employees. It can happen when you're happy or sad, busy or bored. It happens to people of every race and ethnicity, and in every region of the world. It also happens randomly. You just never know when it'll strike. It may strike when you need it most or when you're too busy to notice it. And it happens to you – you certainly can't force it. It just happens. It strikes like a flash and then it's gone. That's why you have to pay attention to it.

Inspiration has the power to transform lives. Paying attention to what inspires you, understanding why it's important to you, and then taking action can lead your life in a direction you never could have imagined.

That's what happened to my dad, Paul Gersper.

My dad turned 80 years old very recently. And he's also about to become a first-time published novelist, at eighty! Writing a novel was not a part of his life plan; he just happened to be inspired by a few small boxes of letters he discovered as the executor of his late aunt's estate. While he gave away, sold, or threw away her remaining possessions according to his aunt's wishes, he felt compelled to take the boxes of letters with him as he returned home. What he discovered in those boxes inspired him to give voice to the now-departed lovers who had written them: his late aunt and uncle.

Here's my dad in his own words explaining what inspired him and why it was so important that he pen Love Letters from the Grave.

"When I discovered the letters, what I noticed first was they were definitely old, and written on all kinds of random paper (factory invoices, time cards, scrap paper, etc), folded very neatly, and obviously important to my aunt. I read a few of them and was so intrigued I knew I needed to read more, but there were too many to read right then. There were four boxes containing a total of about 130 letters, so I decided to take them home with me and read them all.

"I read them all over two or three months, and I was just entranced. I discovered they wrote these letters when they were each in their early forties, and were both happily married at the time – to other people! And yet, they wrote all these amazing love letters to each other. So then I decided to read them all again.

"As I read the letters, I thought about the life of my uncle up to that point. I knew he had been given a life sentence when he was a 15-year-old boy, early in the Great Depression, for driving a get-away car in one of the deadliest bank robberies in the mid-west... And now I was reading love letters he had written to another woman, while he was a happily married family man... As I was reading the letters I started thinking about the two lovers' story; their lives before they met each other; and their life after they married each other. They lived such an inspired life and they loved each other intensely for the whole of the time they were together. I just figured that this was such a tender love story that it had to be shared, as an example that might inspire others.

"It took four to five years from when I first read the letters, to do the research and to write the story. First, I transcribed all the letters exactly as they were written, then I did some detailed research in order to learn about their lives. Most of my research focused on interviewing everyone I could find who knew something about them. After my research was completed, I became even more inspired to write their story, which I first wrote as a biography and then re-wrote as a novel.

"My aunt and uncle lived a life that not only is a personal inspiration to me, but can also be a great inspiration to others, especially to young people. Their lives show us that it's possible for two people to love each other, deeply and tenderly, for their entire lives.

"There are three main themes in the book that I believe are important for readers. First, that personal redemption is possible. My uncle served twenty years in prison and then went on to create a most exemplary life. Second is the value of personal responsibility that our culture fostered in people in the early 1900's. I think more of that is needed in our modern world. And the third theme is the importance of living lightly on our earth. These themes were all deeply engrained in my aunt and uncle's life, and are all woven into a beautiful love story, which I hope will impact the lives of everyone who reads it. I became more and more inspired as I was writing their story; and now, as I near the end of the publication process, I'm very much looking forward to sharing the inspiring love story of Charlie and Molly with others!"

Professor Dr Paul Logan Gersper, Author of Love Letters from the Grave

Matthew B. Gersper, Author and Founder of HappyLiving.com

About the Author

Dr. Paul Logan Gersper is Emeritus Professor of Pedology at the University of California at Berkeley. He joined the Berkeley faculty in 1968, after earning his B.S, M.S., and Ph.D. degrees from The Ohio State University. Taking advantage of the Korean G.I. Bill, he entered Ohio State in 1957, after serving three years as an Army Combat Engineer. He married his wife, Freda, and had their first son, Markham, while in the Army, and then had three more sons, Jeffrey (deceased), Matthew and Michael, and a daughter, Linda, during the ten plus years they attended Ohio State.

Professor Gersper had a successful and varied career at Berkeley. He maintained the largest teaching and student advising loads in his college. He was a faculty athletic advisor and a Peace Corps advisor for approximately 25 years. He also served his college as Department Chairman; Assistant Dean; Vice-Chairman of the Faculty; Undergraduate Program Chairman, and International Visitor Program Director.

His research program focused on soils and ecosystem investigations conducted in different life zones of the United States (including Arctic Alaska and alpine tundras, and eastern deciduous and western coniferous forests) and sustainable agricultural research taking place mainly in the Salinas Valley of California and on the island nation of Cuba.

In Arctic Alaska, he was a member of four research teams: one conducting soils and ecosystem investigations in the Atoms for Peace, Operation Plowshare Program; another monitoring radioactive fallout from nuclear testing by the Soviet Union in Siberia; another researching ecosystems in the International Biological Program, and another undertaking stressed ecosystem research in connection with the building of the Alaskan oil pipeline. In Cuba, he was a member of the first U.S. Scientific Agriculture Delegation to that island nation, and was the team leader of four follow-up delegations investigating Cuba's conversion from chemically-based to organically-based agriculture. In the Salinas valley, he conducted organically-based, sustainable agricultural research, and helped direct a small-farmer training program at the Rural Development Center.

He is the author or co-author of approximately 100 journal articles, book chapters, and research reports, and more than 100 newspaper articles on behalf of Lions Clubs International. He lives with his wife of 61 years in Prescott Valley, Arizona. In addition to their four children they have 10 grandchildren, four great-grandchildren, and five "adopted" grandchildren.

Love Letters from the Grave is his first novel.

Thank You

Thank you for reading Love Letters from the Grave!

If you enjoyed this book, please leave a REVIEW on Amazon!

Join Our Community

Be advised of upcoming books and updates from Happy Living! We are on a mission to improve the health and wellbeing of the world, one person at a time.

Our blog is filled with ideas for living with health, abundance, and compassion.

Go to www.happyliving.com to sign up for our free membership.

Happy Living

Made in the USA
San Bernardino, CA
14 January 2017